# THE DEVIL HAS FOUR FACES

General Fuchs-Ohm did not escape empty-handed from the Allies' marching into Hitler's Germany. He took the secret lists of every American who had contributed support to the Nazi cause.

Now, years later, Fuchs begins to blackmail those who betrayed their country's faith.

He starts with Andrew Strauss, the son of a multimillionaire brewer, Karl Strauss. Unfortunately for Fuchs, he does not know that Denis Blaine, a wartime victim he left for dead, is engaged to Karl Strauss' beautiful niece. And Denis Blaine will stop at nothing to destroy Fuchs . . .

---

**A NOVEL OF SUSPENSE BY AMERICA'S MASTER STORYTELLER**

# ATTENTION: SCHOOLS AND CORPORATIONS

PINNACLE Books are available at quantity discounts with bulk purchases for educational, business or special promotional use. For further details, please write to: SPECIAL SALES MANAGER, Pinnacle Books, Inc., 1430 Broadway, New York, NY 10018.

# WRITE FOR OUR FREE CATALOG

If there is a Pinnacle Book you want—and you cannot find it locally—it is available from us simply by sending the title and price plus 75¢ to cover mailing and handling costs to:

>Pinnacle Books, Inc.
>Reader Service Department
>1430 Broadway
>New York, NY 10018

Please allow 6 weeks for delivery.

_____Check here if you want to receive our catalog regularly.

# THE DEVIL HAS FOUR FACES

# JOHN JAKES

**A TOM DOHERTY ASSOCIATES BOOK**
*Distributed by Pinnacle Books, New York*

*To Ben and Mary Faulkner
and the days of
The Great Rib Cage*

This is a work of fiction. All the characters and events portrayed in this book are fictional, and any resemblance to real people or incidents is purely coincidental.

THE DEVIL HAS FOUR FACES

Copyright © 1958 by Thomas Bouregy & Company

All rights reserved, including the right to reproduce this book or portions thereof in any form.

A Tor Book

First printing: October 1981

ISBN: 0-523-48013-X

Cover illustration by Richard Coyne.

Printed in the United States of America

Distributed by Pinnacle Books, New York.

"I charge thee, Satan, housed within this man,
 To yield possession to my holy prayers
 And to thy state of darkness hie thee straight:
 I conjure thee by all the saints in heaven!"

*—The Comedy of Errors*

# CHAPTER I

The sky began to shake with the rumble of the Allied bombers coming again.

The long windows flanked by luxurious wine-velvet draperies presented a grim view of the city of Berlin. Long plumes of smoke, still-smoldering signal fires of last night's destruction, trailed into the darkening yellow heavens. Patterns of searchlights flicked across the bellies of low-hanging clouds, searching the night for the invader. A siren cried in an adjoining street. Around the corner of an intersection visible from the windows of the third-floor apartment scurried an elderly woman on a bicycle, head instinctively drawn down in the gloom. The antiaircraft batteries chattered alive, followed by first detonations, as sticks of explosives rained down.

Hauptmann Erwin Kloder regarded the scene with mounting panic. Stained fingers pressed still another cigarette between his lips. He started violently at the sound of his superior's voice just at his elbow:

"So again they attack, Erwin. I admire their persistence."

Kloder turned a worried face toward the man in the full-dress uniform of the High Command standing beside him. The most exalted orders and decorations of the Nazi government glittered on the man's tunic. "The city cannot continue to suffer this punishment," Kloder stated softly. "Berlin is ruined, dead. And so, I am afraid, is our government."

General Reinhard Fuchs-Ohm chuckled softly. "Surely during the past year you've resigned yourself to this fate, my friend." He clapped his aide on the shoulder. "Fortunate, too, the day you received your assignment, because of all the thousands of fools dying in a misguided orgy of final patriotism, only we shall be free to forge a victory out of the rubble." Fuchs-Ohm snapped his fingers as another series of detonations rocked the windows. "The curtains. We must depart shortly. I have ordered my plane ready for take-off at the airdrome thirty minutes after the all-clear sounds."

"Tonight, General—?" began Kloder with some reluctance.

"Yes, tonight!" Fuchs-Ohm retorted. "Already we have delayed too long."

Responding to the relentless air of command which surrounded Fuchs-Ohm like an intangible cloud, Kloder busied himself with the draperies in the sumptuous apartment. Then he lighted several lamps. "Pack only a light valise for each of us," Fuchs-Ohm called through the open doorway of his study. "We shall have to secure entirely new wardrobes when we reach Switzerland."

Ten minutes later, Kloder emerged from his superior's bedroom and placed a pair of expensive leather attaché cases on the settee. Approaching the entrance to the study, he paused and waited tactfully. Fuchs-Ohm ransacked the bottom drawer of his desk and drew forth three items. One, a gleaming loaded Luger, he tossed to his aide. The mate he thrust out of sight beneath his own tunic. The last article he unrolled with a flourish.

Fuchs-Ohm studied the faded poster, which presented a brightly lithographed figure in dress tails, mustached and bearded, eyes gleaming, while around the head and shoulders arose a flock of flowers, ghosts, rabbits, silks, and cards. *Herr Cagliostro*, ran the legend. *Ein international berühmter Zauberer der Jede Nacht 14-21 September*.

"Perhaps those days when I was poor, giving performances each night, were the happiest of my life," Fuchs-Ohm said softly. "In any event . . ." He folded the poster flat and handed it to Kloder. "In my case, please, Erwin, as one last souvenir of Germany. . . ."

As Kloder returned from packing the memento, the whine of a bomb cut shrilly down the sky, perilously close. The explosion shook the walls. A lamp with a delicate porcelain base fell from an end table and shattered on the floor.

"We are escaping not a minute too soon—if we make it at all," breathed Kloder.

Fuchs-Ohm inspected the desk a final time and extinguished the lamp in the study. Kloder repeated his ritual of reminding his superior of things which otherwise might go forgotten:

"Funds, General?"

Fuchs-Ohm drew his officer's overcoat from a foyer closet. "Awaiting us at my bank in Geneva. Placed there two and a half years ago, when it became apparent that Germany would lose this war. You see, Erwin," the general continued, strolling to the marble fireplace and gazing up at a painting of Adolf Hitler framed in heavy ornamental gilt, "only you share my secret. Only you realize that I much prefer living to dying for a cause which has failed." He scowled contemptuously at the rather pompous, pink-cheeked image of the black-haired man with the small mustache and the swastika arm band. "Long ago, every German officer should have recognized the signs of his impending madness." Fuchs-Ohm spat on the floor below the painting. "Who wishes to die for a lunatic?"

Kloder coughed discreetly. "The . . . ah . . . records, General?"

"Ah, yes, the key to our fortunes. With the funds

# THE DEVIL HAS FOUR FACES

I have managed to swindle from our confused government, and with those records, we shall make a handsome killing." Fuchs-Ohm paced the apartment, checking for final articles he might wish to take along. "Goebbels is a wretched little man, but working under him had one advantage—access to the secret lists of every citizen of the United States who remained loyal to the fatherland, and who contributed funds to our cause." One of the general's eyebrows lifted in cold mirth. "But the records—one thin volume—also await us across the Swiss border. I arranged to have the precious book smuggled there less than a week ago." He cocked his head. "The explosions are dwindling. What last details remain?"

"The prisoners, General. The two Americans."

"Oh, yes, I almost forgot. The two captured intelligence agents who parachuted behind the lines three weeks ago. Their interrogation had been proceeding nicely. But no choice is left. Any information they possess would be useless now. Goebbels thought I might be able to devote more attention to their questioning if they were locked in the garret of my flat." He motioned to Kloder, who followed him into the hall.

Fuchs-Ohm stood on tiptoe and seized a chain hanging from the ceiling. He tugged, and a wooden stairway swung down. Kloder made a face. "Phew! What a stench." Fuchs-Ohm called for a flashlight, and the two men ascended into the dark garret with its miasmal odor of confinement.

The beam of light outlined a pair of tattered and dirty figures. Both Americans blinked against the light. The faces, arms, and shoulders of the men showed horrible disfigurement—a result of certain of the general's interrogation practices which employed fire and the knife. One of the prisoners, a blond, stocky young man, made an abortive effort to rush his captor. Kloder whipped out his Luger. "Keep back!" he snarled.

With a regretful air, Fuchs-Ohm spoke: "Herr Quigley and Herr Blaine, I regret very much that our association must end. But I am leaving the country. Before I departed, however, I wanted to wish you Godspeed and good fortune upon your return to your homeland."

The dark-haired American crouched against the wall, suspicion mingled with hatred in his sunken eyes. The stocky Quigley registered exactly the opposite emotion. His face lit with hope, with the sick and ravaged ghost of a smile.

At that instant, Fuchs-Ohm returned the smile, drew his Luger and shot Quigley in the face. Quigley shrieked briefly and flopped onto his back. Blood streamed down over the bridge of his nose to mingle with the straw and dirt.

The other American, Blaine, rose slightly, his face demented by rage and hatred. "If you are leaving, why did you have to kill him?" The pitch of his voice heightened shrilly. "Why, you filthy—" Suddenly the American doubled both fists and shook them violently in the cone of light from the flash. "He saved my life in Africa! Why did you kill him?" The words blended into a single frenzied cry as Blaine lunged across the straw.

Kloder withdrew apprehensively, ready to shoot, his hand trembling slightly. Fuchs-Ohm fired, his face muscles contorting in spasmodic pleasure.

Gagging and moaning, Blaine crawled off toward the wall. Blood smeared his chest through the tatters of his shirt. He braced himself on the floor, turned one last gaze of pure hatred at the German general, and then sagged face down. Fuchs-Ohm waited a moment and then snapped out the light.

Back in the study, Kloder lifted a telephone from its cradle and swiftly dialed a number. Fuchs-Ohm paced nervously as his aide studied his wristwatch. When four minutes had elapsed, Kloder whispered: "The car will be waiting now, General." Kloder snatched up the two valises and the door slammed, leaving the apartment quiet.

From far away came the last bursts of antiaircraft fire. From the crack where the pull-down stairs met the ceiling, a drop of blood fell, and then another, and still another, staining the marble floor of the deserted house. A feeble groan sounded from the garret. Then silence. After a long while the blood no longer dripped.

One morning several years later, General Reinhard Fuchs-Ohm awoke with sunlight in his eyes and rolled over with a lazy, contented sigh. He rose leisurely from his straw pallet, stretched and drew on a worn shirt and a pair of tattered white trousers. Slipping his feet into woven sandals, he took down the water gourd from its place on the wall of the rude clay house, sloshed a quantity of the tepid liquid in his mouth and spat it onto the dirt floor. A roach scuttled out of sight beneath the pallet. Fuchs-Ohm leaned forward and peered from the window.

Within the fenced enclosure, Consuegra knelt milking the goat. Her black hair gleamed in the sunlight. She had been hardly a child when Fuchs-Ohm first arrived in this remote and sparsely settled part of Mexico. Today the harsh sunlight gleamed on the firm, rounded flesh of a young woman's arm. With a brief sigh, Fuchs-Ohm turned away. Perhaps, he reflected, Erwin Kloder had shown more foresight in entering no such alliance. . . .

Kneeling in the corner, Fuchs-Ohm took a small silver key from a chain about his neck and unlocked a large green metal strongbox. Within the box rested his Luger and his folded poster, as well as a slender leather-bound volume. Flicking open the first page, he read one section of the closely written German script: *Andrew Strauss,* the entry commenced. The name was followed by that of a large American city. *Brewery owner.* Next, the figure of thirty thousand dollars had been entered opposite

# THE DEVIL HAS FOUR FACES

a date, and the final line of the entry read: *Deposited through the International Bank of Buenos Aires.*

Snapping shut the volume, Fuchs-Ohm withdrew the last article, a newspaper, and relocked the lid. Poor Andrew Strauss, he thought. Secretly loyal to the little madman, devoutly and deviously contributing to the cause of Nazi Germany. Would Andrew Strauss have been so eager to contribute if he had realized that years after the little madman died in his bunker, the ghosts of hidden loyalty would rise again?

The Strauss entry represented only one of hundreds. Fuchs-Ohm stared past Consuegra and her bleating goat to the purplish crests of the mountains rising jaggedly in the north. Beyond those crests lay America, rich with wealth for the man clever enough to take it.

Fuchs-Ohm lit a thin cigar and unfolded the newspaper, a Dallas edition. More than a month old, it nevertheless contained indications that the hour had struck for Fuchs-Ohm to enter America. Prosperity and spending had zoomed to new heights. Every industry—like the brewery of Andrew Strauss—enjoyed heightened prosperity. Fuchs-Ohm tossed the paper aside and called to Consuegra from the hut's entrance.

Her teeth flashed a smile and she waved. "In a moment, *querido.*"

Bending to her task with the goat, Consuegra

heard the scuff of his sandals in dust. She raised her dark eyes, smiling. Fuchs-Ohm bent forward.

In disbelief and terror she attempted to rise. The pail of milk slopped over. Deftly Fuchs-Ohm punctured the fabric of her blouse and imbedded a slender knife in the brown firmness of her breast. Then he stood off until her eyes closed and her bare, dusty feet ceased thrashing. He withdrew his knife, knotted a fist in her hair and dragged her into the house.

Her uncles would not arrive for their monthly visit for two weeks. By that time he would be well gone. For a brief space, he regarded her corpse lying on the dirt floor. How wide, how startled and frightened her eyes had been at the moment of the knife's impact. Her love, he felt, had been genuine and selfless, and for a second he experienced a touch of regret. Then his gaze caught the rising line of purple, promising mountains to the north, and he ran into the yard, clutching his box, and climbed onto the tethered burro. Kneeing the beast with authority, he set off down the dusty road.

Less than two kilometers distant, Erwin Kloder lived in a similar dwelling. Kloder hailed him eagerly in the sunlight.

"Today, General?" he exclaimed.

"Yes. The American pilot of wetbacks landed in the hills last night, to talk. He will meet us at the village and fly us over the border tonight. For an extra sum—highly exorbitant—I arranged to pro-

# THE DEVIL HAS FOUR FACES

cure identification papers which will prevent our being captured as aliens and returned to this country. The pilot will also furnish us with clothing."

Kloder brought his own burro to the front of the hut. Fuchs-Ohm wondered idly why he had never disposed of this faithful man, and completed the rather new and startling thought with the conclusion that thus far he had clearly found no valid reason for doing so. Innocent of such considerations, Kloder swung a quizzical eye back along the route by which Fuchs-Ohm had arrived.

"How did Consuegra take your departure, General?"

Fuchs-Ohm also turned, and noticed with curiosity that a dark, evil-appearing flock of birds whirled and dipped just over the brow of the horizon. A thin smile etched his features. "There is your answer, Erwin."

Kloder offered no comment. The two men set off down the road toward the village, dust rising from the paths of the burros in the morning sunlight. Two men riding side by side could hardly have been more similar: of nearly identical stature and facial structure, they appeared to be twin figures against the bright landscape.

# CHAPTER II

Denis Blaine measured two ounces of Chivas Regal Scotch whisky into a sparkling tumbler and drank it neat. For the tenth time, he completed a last adjustment of his white tie before the mirror, slipped into his overcoat and—rather self-consciously—his Homburg, and left his apartment.

Steering his convertible through the smoky fall twilight, he reflected that he had no business entertaining such forebodings as now plagued him. After all, just what the devil did he fear? On the basis of a single dream he had constructed a scaffolding of nerves which threatened to box him in. It was foolish. He had, first of all, survived the war with little more than the faint image of a once-brutal scar over his right ribs, and his road since returning to civilian life had climbed steadily upward. He prided himself on the fact that he had built it alone, without help.

His English mother could only offer good wishes and not cold cash when opportunity arose for Denis

# THE DEVIL HAS FOUR FACES

to buy a small interest in one of the city's better offset printing firms. Through study and shrewd management, Denis had acquired control of the company and built a reputation for the finest printing within a radius of a thousand miles. With three major beer brewers located in the city, all operating on generous national advertising budgets, Denis found himself eight years after his mother's death with more business than he could handle.

Finally, through contacts connected with the unromantic process of producing brochures by the millions, he met the niece of Karl Strauss, crusty old founder of Strauss Beer, which ranked second in national sales. At the end of his road of hard work stood his reward—the most wonderful girl in the world, Diana Meadows.

The thought of his fiancée somewhat diverted him from memory of his dream—an affair dealing with his last hours in a foul attic room belonging to a master of butchery. The dream had its foundations in reality, but the reality itself possessed the qualities of nightmare, full of shadows, bad smells, screaming and pain and the crash-crash-crash of the city of Berlin falling into ruin.

He called for Diana at her apartment and escorted her to the car. Her copper hair gleamed in the muted lights shining about the building's portico. Her face presented a mischievous innocence belied by her womanly figure, which was never more apparent than tonight. In the car, she tucked the folds of her pink sheath gown around her legs, adjusted her fur wrap, and leaned forward to kiss Denis firmly and passionately. He delayed starting the car for a moment, and when at last he did, they set off with a jerky motion.

"Never kiss me in heavy traffic," Denis said, grinning. "That would be a sure route to the hospital."

Laughing softly, Diana leaned back. "Are you nervous? I hope not."

"I feel like the sacrificial sheep about to be placed on the altar stone."

"Now, my family isn't such a bad bunch . . ."

"No, your uncle is a fine old man," Denis agreed. "The other member does not arouse . . . let's say . . . frantic admiration."

"Oh, Andrew is a good-natured sort." A frown marred Diana's forehead slightly. "Or at least he used to be. When he took over control of Strauss Beer six months ago, everyone thought sales would double. Perhaps triple. Strangely, he has been— well, no one can explain it. He's turned surly. Do you ever notice the way he chews his nails? That began six months ago."

"Um." Denis switched on the radio.

A disc jockey's unctuous tones announced an old favorite, a dance arrangement known familiarly in English at the end of the war as *You Are the One*.

After a moment Diana noticed that Denis scowled.

"Is the music too tame, darling? I don't know

# THE DEVIL HAS FOUR FACES

whether we can get Fat Henry and his Kings of Dixieland at this hour . . ."

Absently, Denis shook his head. "No. I remember they played that song a lot in Berlin, after the liberation. It's a German drinking song, I think."

Diana reached out with one gloved hand and switched off the bubbling melody. "Darling, you have the strangest expression on your face . . ."

As he did. At thirty-one, Denis Blaine's face suggested a calm nature, reserved friendliness, and a great deal of steady purpose. In the yellowish gleams of the dashboard lights, however, his face had slipped into a mask of near-anguish. He inclined his whole body forward toward the wheel, as if straining against an unseen terror behind him.

"What is it, darling?"

"Nothing," he muttered. "Ridiculous . . ."

She placed one gloved hand on his arm. "You're not telling me the truth."

Denis braked for a stoplight and placed a cigarette between his lips, exhaling in short, agitated puffs. "Well, perhaps if I spilled it, some of the nonsense would blow away. But the entire business is absurd!" he protested again.

"Would you be saying that so vehemently if you didn't believe the opposite?" Diana asked, her voice warm with affection and concern.

After a pause, Denis said reluctantly, "You remember the story of how my friend Quigley and I were sent on an intelligence mission near the end of the war? We parachuted behind the enemy lines, were captured, and taken to Berlin, turned over to a General Fuchs-Ohm for questioning. For torture, actually." Diana nodded. "Well, as I've told you, this Nazi shot Quigley, killed him for no good reason. He shot me, too, leaving me for dead. When I was finally rescued—by Allied troops searching the place—I had gone nearly out of my mind. Quigley had saved my life once, and the American soldiers had to tie and drag me to a hospital because I kept screaming that I would kill General Fuchs-Ohm. Or so I was told."

In the quiet throbbing of the motor, Diana nodded again. She had listened to the account several times previously, and knew each agonizing twist and turn. She felt his suffering as hers, even now.

"After the war, I forgot about General Fuchs-Ohm," Denis continued. "Like so many things in wartime—quick love affairs, quick friendships—the emotions had to be forgotten while making up for all the lost years afterward. I seldom think of General Fuchs-Ohm any more."

Again Denis paused.

"But last night," he said slowly, "I dreamed of him again."

"Could there be any reason for the dream?" Diana asked. "A reason you could explain?"

"Yes," said Denis, "and no."

"You mean because—as I remember—the general never turned up after the war? He simply disappeared. The Allies wanted to try him for war crimes and were unable to locate him."

"But I have known that for a long time," Denis said. "So many years have passed . . . Just in the last few days, I must have seen or heard something which told me I would meet him again. Because I seldom think of him any more, it took a dream to bring the premonition to life." He laughed with faint bitterness. "Know any good head-shrinkers?"

"I wish I did," Diana replied half-jestingly, then bit her lip. "What a fool I am! Giving you flip answers when the problem really troubles you. But honestly, Denis, I have no solution."

"That's the hell of it," Denis breathed. "Neither have I."

Quickly he swung the wheel, nearly overshooting the iron gates which mounted a low landscaped hill to the home of Karl Strauss.

The Strauss mansion piled against the darkening sky in a maze of turrets, battlements, and wooden gingerbread decoration, a remnant of the early days when the brewery kings pyramided sudden fortunes and displayed their wealth ostentatiously. Tonight, its windows threw a blaze of light across the treetops of the suburb of Briarwood, which contained the homes of several of the most wealthy citizens of the nation. Denis always felt a certain warmth and friendliness whenever he visited the place, primarily because of the genial personality of old Karl Strauss, who had risen from an immigrant vat cleaner in another man's brewery to become a millionaire.

Denis parked his convertible on the slope of the curving drive, and he and Diana climbed the steps toward the dinner party both of them had come to dread just a bit.

In a sumptuous upper bedroom of the mansion, Andrew Strauss burned his fingers on the cigar he was lighting when the private telephone on his nightstand let forth a jarring, insistent jangle. He lifted the receiver with a trembling hand. "Hello?"

"Mr. Strauss?" inquired a faintly apologetic male voice. "Harry Soames calling."

Andrew sank down on the edge of the bed. His stout, rather pasty face shone abruptly with gleaming beads of sweat. "I asked you never to telephone me here!" he said, a touch of desperation in his voice. "And I know why you have called." Torn by indecision, he went on, "I simply do not have the money yet."

"Your payment is already eight days overdue," replied Soames. "Please understand, Mr. Strauss, that this is just my job. I get orders, and I have to check up. I told my . . . contact . . . that you were temporarily strapped, but—"

"This devil you work for fails to realize that I haven't yet inherited Strauss Beer!" Andrew shot back. "I still receive a salary from my father's cor-

# THE DEVIL HAS FOUR FACES

poration, and this month I have already overextended myself. The money is not available."

"The man I work for—"

"Who is this mysterious somebody?" Strauss raged. "Have him call me in person!"

Soames responded unhappily: "You know I can't say anything about him. But I told him that you said you were out of funds. He pointed out that in nineteen forty-two you managed to scrape together thirty thousand dollars which you deposited with the International Bank of Buenos Aires. Remember? I showed you a photostat of a page from a book written in German, showing the entry. I don't know any more than that, but he said you would understand."

As always happened when he heard the name of that remote banking firm in South America, Andrew Strauss turned pale.

"I am supposed to come to your home in three days," Soames explained. "I will make the collection then. Good night, Mr. Strauss."

"Wait a second!"

"Sorry, but I just carry out orders," explained the unhappy voice.

"Wait!" repeated Andrew. "Wait, damn you!"

"In three days, Mr. Strauss. Goodbye."

The connection clicked dead.

Andrew Strauss stumbled into the room adjoining his bedroom, flicked on the lights and poured himself a stiff shot of bourbon. Dimly he recalled that he was due downstairs for a dinner party. He dreaded the affair, as he dreaded his entire existence. Ever since that first phone call from Soames, life for Andrew had been a nightmare.

Just past forty, a bachelor, and not bad looking in spite of his soft, rather pallid complexion and his stout frame, Andrew Strauss should have been quite satisfied with his position in the world. Inevitable inheritor of a mammoth business enterprise, he had more money than he needed. This mansion would eventually belong to him, together with controlling stock in Strauss Beer and numerous other holdings.

As he returned to the bedroom and forced his shaking fingers to manipulate the studs of his dress shirt, a cold clamminess claimed his body. The excuse he had fabricated for Soames was the product of indecision, an effort to stall for time. He had money aplenty to make the payment, but his endurance was rubbing thin.

Andrew slipped into his dinner jacket and, stepping to the mirror, studied his face. He said to the reflected face: "You really don't look much like a murderer. But then, a man can only be pushed to a certain point, as Mr. Soames is going to find out three days from now."

Eyes oddly glazed, Andrew Strauss left the room. Unknowingly he bit at one of his fingernails as he descended the long stairway toward the guests who had already assembled. In three days . . .

The genial patriarch of the Strauss family greeted Denis and Diana in the foyer, while the butler fumbled in the background, constantly dismayed by the old millionaire's lack of formality. A nearly perfect representation of the jolly German burgher, old Karl Strauss wore rumpled black evening dress over his corporation, deliberately maintained his old-world accent and delighted in his mop of white hair and his reddish cheeks.

"The favorite niece," he said, "and Denis. Come in, both of you." He slapped Denis on the back and chuckled. "Beer before dinner? Or one of those miserable highball concoctions? Only under the influence of young people do I allow such potions served in my home. This way, into the library. A few guests—Hemmerfring, my production vice-president, his wife, some others—you'll meet them all."

Spirits somewhat raised by the genial chatter of the portly old man, Denis and Diana passed through the hallway of the massive old house and into the library where the party was commencing. Andrew Strauss grunted an offhand greeting and retired to one corner, frowning into an undiluted glass of bourbon. Shortly the company retired to the long candlelit dining room for a fine dinner.

As coffee was being served, Karl Strauss pulled a

piece of paper from his pocket and passed it to Diana, seated at his right. "I thought we might have some entertainment after dinner," he boomed. "I engaged this fellow. Understand he's excellent. I have always been fascinated by conjurors."

Diana studied the printed sheet, then passed it to Denis. The copy on the sheet announced the talents of Cagliostro the Magician, available for theatres and private parties.

Denis examined the face framed in an oval design on the circular. Then he turned white.

Diana gasped, "Darling, what's wrong?"

Old Karl Strauss, conversing loudly with Hemmerfring, seated on the opposite side of the table, boomed, "You like conjurors, too, Hemmerfring? Wonderful. Yes, I understand Mr. Fuchs has arrived. We will all go into the music room for the performance."

Denis licked his lips. His stomach ached with the force of suddenly renewed emotion. One finger stabbed at the portrait. "Now I remember, Diana. I saw this flyer four days ago, lying on a table in the library, on the afternoon I picked you up here for dinner. This is what caused the dream."

Denis stared bleakly. "That face." A muscle in his throat throbbed spasmodically in the candlelight. Against the background of fashionably dressed men and women chattering gayly in a gleam of sparkling crystal, Denis looked pale and shaken.

# THE DEVIL HAS FOUR FACES

Diana shuddered when she met his eyes and saw the expression in them.

"This is the same face," he whispered. "This is the general." Denis overturned his chair as he stood up. "Mr. Strauss?" he said in a tight voice.

Old Karl Strauss turned. "Eh? Yes, my boy?"

"The magician—this Cagliostro—you say he has arrived?"

"Why, I believe so. I was told he had gone into the kitchen for his meal."

Diana leaned forward and gripped Denis' hand. "Denis, please!"

Denis threw off her hand, stalked from the dining room and flung the doors shut behind him with a crash.

Mr. Richard Fuchs, professionally billed as Cagliostro the Magician and immaculately attired in full evening dress, finished his cup of tea in the large, well-lighted kitchen of the Karl Strauss mansion. A haughty servant bustled through swinging doors and announced, "I believe Mr. Strauss and his guests will be ready for your performance in just a few minutes." Fuchs inclined his head pleasantly.

He commented on the excellent meal he had been served and questioned the servant as to where he might prepare his equipment for the show. The servant irritably cleared a section of a large worktable. Fuchs thanked him profusely. The buxom cook watched avidly, her eyes round with curiosity. Fuchs slung his suitcase onto the table with a flourish, opened the lid and drew forth a purple silk robe.

He slipped into the garment, inspecting the voluminous sleeves for certain apparatus necessary to his act. The silken material bore an intricate pattern of decorations in gold thread, including moons, planets, and other astrological signs. Fuchs rifled quickly through the contents of his case to make certain that each piece of equipment was in its assigned place.

He conducted this inspection mechanically. Secretly the mind of this man who had been engaged for an evening of entertainment seethed with speculation. He really had no business venturing into this household. A contact handled all transactions with the victim, but a streak of cruelty in the magician's make-up demanded that he view the suffering object of his plan at first hand. With a sense of exhilaration, Fuchs snapped the case and lighted a cigarette. From the mammoth copper-hooded stove came the aroma of a freshly brewed pot of tea.

Fuchs turned, melting the cook with the warmth of his smile. "I wonder," he said in his carefully contrived accent, "whether I might have another cup of that delicious tea."

The cook blushed and poured the requested cup. As he reached to take it, he heard the flap of the

# THE DEVIL HAS FOUR FACES

swinging doors behind him, then a hard, quiet voice:

"Mr. Cagliostro?"

By a massive effort, the magician kept his facial muscles composed and even affixed a puzzled smile upon his lips as he turned. "Yes?"

The magician's eyes probed the face of the young man framed in the doorway, fists balled at his sides. Instantly Fuchs jumped the time barrier, surrounding the face in his mind's eye with the yellow circle of a flashlight's glow. Like a grisly memory came the foul stench of a closed garret.

The cook dropped a kettle. A nerve in Fuchs' right cheek twitched. The crashing utensil had sounded for one frantic instant like the report of a bomb out of the sky.

"We have not had the pleasure of an introduction, I'm afraid," he said smoothly.

Denis Blaine stalked forward. He threw a pointed glance at the cook, who withdrew hastily.

Then Denis took a deep breath. "We met several years ago in Berlin. We met in your apartment. Isn't that correct, General?"

Struggling to maintain his composure, Fuchs folded the purple gown across the gleaming bosom of his dress shirt and belted the robe so that his evening dress was completely concealed. Carelessly drawing the cigarette from between his lips, he studied his polished black shoes and flicked ashes down at them.

"My dear young man," he said, "we have never met and I have never been a general. I served in the United States Army with the rank of sergeant, and if you would care to see my identification . . ."

"Shut up," Denis said flatly. "I wanted to kill you in Berlin, General. Now we meet by chance and I remind you of Jim Quigley, the man you shot without a reason, you filthy—" Denis raised his hands, trembling. Fuchs stood immobile as the young man's fingers halted scant inches from his throat.

"See!" Fuchs whispered, a tiny smile tugging at his mouth. "The years have changed you, my friend. Murder is not so easy as it seemed in Berlin." Little lights of triumph played in the eyes of the magician. "I am helpless, at your mercy. Yet you are powerless. In Berlin the animal side of your nature held sway. Tonight you belong to a more civilized way of life, and it makes you weak."

A vein on Denis' temple throbbed visibly. With a muttered curse, he dropped his hands, wheeled and slammed from the kitchen. Angry footsteps retreated down the corridor and died away.

Only then did Fuchs lean weakly against the wall and drag forth a handkerchief to wipe the cold perspiration from his own forehead.

"Close," he whispered. "Very, very close."

Apparently the American was a guest in this house. What a damned unlucky chance, ruining his plans in such a fashion. With even one person

# THE DEVIL HAS FOUR FACES

making lunatic accusations, he was subject to suspicion. A covered trail ranked as his foremost weapon, and that young American who had come within scant inches of murdering him possessed dangerous information.

Fuchs breathed with relief now, for he had been uncertain that Denis Blaine did not actually possess the drive to kill. Fuchs had gambled, but his victory was slim. If the American remained in the audience tonight and in a day or two began to make an investigation into the background of Richard Fuchs, that would prove a serious threat. What's more, he could not flee. That would be an admission of guilt.

Quickly the magician made his decision.

He opened his case again and nervously examined two items of equipment he regularly used to climax his performance. Tonight he must insert the stunt early in the program. He rummaged in a drawer until he found a short-handled sharp-bladed kitchen knife. He hoped fervently that no one would interrupt him until he could put his plan into motion. Touching the front of his robe, he glanced around and fixed his eyes upon a fluorescent lighting bracket in the ceiling. He clenched his teeth as the swinging doors flapped open.

Breathy with panic, Fuchs palmed the knife, straightened his robe and spun around. "Mr. Fuchs, the guests are ready," the haughty butler said.

# CHAPTER III

Conversation rippled at an excited pitch as the dinner guests trooped into the music room. Diana, chained by circumstances to the balding and voluble vice-president, Hemmerfring, searched with her eyes for Denis, while Hemmerfring blithely detailed her with endless chatter about the brewing business: ". . . and so I feel superbly confident, Miss Meadows, that when we introduce Strauss Old Times Ale on a nationwide basis, we shall be immensely successful. We have conducted extensive market tests, you know. Columbus, Schenectady, Bakersfield—all very reliable centers. Oh, my yes. Why public acceptance is bound . . ."

"Wonderful," Diana breathed in desperation. She muttered an excuse and dashed past Andrew Strauss—locating a chair for one of the city's leading widows, a Mrs. Grosswin—toward the piano where Denis stood staring into space. She seized his hand.

"Denis . . ." Her lips refused to form the words which touched her heart with cold dread.

## THE DEVIL HAS FOUR FACES

"Yes," Denis whispered. "Yes! He is the man." Savagely he flung his cigarette on the floor. "If I had one more chance . . ." His face twisted.

Diana heard her uncle speak loudly to all those assembled. On the pretext of listening, she faced the group and attempted to stand casually next to Denis, feigning interest in Karl Strauss' words.

"My good friends, I am sure we shall all be delighted by the performance. May I present our guest tonight—Cagliostro the Magician!"

Through a curtained entrance at the opposite side of the room stepped a man carrying a good-sized black suitcase. He bowed low in the face of a spatter of polite applause. Advancing to the center of the marble floor, he smiled as his deft hands unfolded a pair of legs, apparently from out of the bottom of the case. Setting his apparatus upright, he paused momentarily and swung his eyes over the group. He flicked past Denis without stopping. Diana stole a glance at her fiancé. His face had become even paler, and he watched the man called Cagliostro with a terrible concentration.

"May I show you, ladies and gentlemen," said the magician, placing a candle in a holder upon the closed top of his case, "an unusual and perplexing candle which I acquired in Turkey? I light it thus." Cagliostro applied a match to the tip, and brought forth a black cloth. He dropped the cloth over the lighted taper, carefully opened a slit in the material and allowed only the burning tip of the candle to peep through. "My candle is exceptionally accommodating, you see, because it understands that I am very lazy and does not require that I blow it out when I am ready to retire. Merely a flick . . ." The supple wrists whipped the cloth into the air. Candleholder, burning taper and all had vanished.

The guests responded with warm applause. Even Andrew Strauss lost his glazed expression long enough to clap. Without a break, the magician moved into his next stunt, which involved producing a full goldfish bowl from thin air.

Diana studied the mysterious figure standing before the seated semicircle of onlookers. Against the old-rose wallpaper and black draperies of the room, he presented a commanding and powerful figure as he swept the crowd with hard blue eyes. He had a savagely pronged nose, and sleek hair gleamed pure white beneath the glittering blaze of a massive chandelier. Despite his hair, he did not strike Diana as an old man. Through his remotely heard words, he radiated—for Diana—an aura of savage power, heightened by the weird purple robe he wore. The surface of the robe literally crawled with peculiar and faintly evil designs which she only half-recognized. The robe covered him from neck to shoe tips, and by closing her eyes the merest trace, Diana could imagine him as some ancient necromancer towering against a blood-red sky, his hands supple and dangerous, flying in the air like living things,

# THE DEVIL HAS FOUR FACES

his eyes cruelly bright and strangely out of place above his carefully forged smile. Abruptly, as if tuned to her fiancé's mind, she hated Cagliostro the Magician, hated him as an extremely deadly and ruthless animal . . .

"Permit me to show you a very old weapon." Diana snapped back to reality as the magician produced an old-fashioned pistol from his case, a heavy antique muzzle-loader fired with a percussion cap. Its gleaming metal had been lovingly preserved.

As if a current of electricity had passed through the room, the guests leaned forward and the air hung heavy with a tense silence. A distant danger signal began to clang in Diana's mind.

"In all the recorded history of the magic art," Cagliostro spoke, his voice rising hypnotically under the glittering crystal chandelier, "one demonstration has fascinated and confounded the greatest brains of the civilized world. This demonstration, fraught with peril, involves firing a loaded pistol at a human target, and an attempt on the part of the man serving as the target to bend and warp the forces of space sufficiently so that he may slow the death-dealing bullet. In brief, ladies and gentlemen, I shall attempt to catch a bullet between my teeth here tonight, defying the laws of nature by the naked force of my will. I am never certain whether I shall succeed but"—a half-smile—"with your very kind indulgence, I shall try."

Diana Meadows flashed another look at Denis Blaine, and found him staring at the pistol with morbid concentration.

Cagliostro himself seemed in the grip of tension. Perspiration beaded his face and he spoke through teeth held tightly together.

"This pistol belonged originally to Professor Anderson, the Wizard of the North, a Scotsman who introduced this very dangerous demonstration to the music halls of the world. The pistol passed to Herrmann the Great, and thence to his chief assistant, William Robinson. In nineteen eighteen, Robinson appeared at the Royal Regent Theatre in London under the name Chung Ling Soo, and on the stage of that theatre he was shot to death by this very pistol, performing the feat I shall attempt before your eyes. No man since Robinson has dared use this weapon. But tonight I shall put it to the test."

Cagliostro paused, his eyelids fluttering in a peculiar, dazed fashion. Then he regained his poise and continued: "I shall require a volunteer to fire the pistol at my head." Another pause. "Who would like to assist me in this experiment?"

Like the stroke of doom Diana heard a voice reply:

"*I would.*"

Denis Blaine stepped forward, his face rigid, his hands clenched along the seams of his trousers.

Cagliostro smiled icily. He thanked Denis and

circulated among the members of the audience, allowing them to examine a bullet. Then he passed the bullet to Denis, together with a penknife. "Please scratch a mark upon the bullet," instructed the magician. "Any sort of mark you wish, but one which will enable the bullet to be positively identified." Denis accepted the knife and drew the point across the shell to form a six-pointed star. Cagliostro again circulated the bullet for examination.

Nearly out of her wits with terror, Diana at last grasped the cruelty of the plan. Knowing that Denis could not summon courage to commit murder, the ex-Nazi intended to goad and torture him with a ripe opportunity. But with equal suddenness, Diana wondered whether Denis could refrain, given this terrible chance.

Old Karl Strauss leaned forward, a frown worrying his forehead.

"Please examine the pistol," Cagliostro said, handing the weapon to Denis.

Carefully Denis inspected the weapon. His eyes flicked upward an instant before he handed it back. "I believe it could kill a man," he agreed softly.

The magician poured a charge of black powder down the muzzle. He inserted paper wadding and produced from the folds of his robe an ornamental ramrod marked with circular grooves. Quickly he tamped down the wadding and extended the pistol vertically to Denis.

"Please drop the bullet in."

Denis obeyed. Under the electric fire of the chandelier, his face shone with a moist film. Cagliostro rammed the bullet home, and then tamped down an additional quantity of wadding with the opposite end of the decorated rod. He gripped the pistol by its barrel and offered it to Denis, who took it. Cagliostro, ramrod still in hand, retreated a dozen paces and picked up a small plate. He straightened his shoulders. Diana's heartbeat nearly deafened her.

"May we have absolute quiet?" the magician requested.

He smiled at Denis Blaine.

"Please raise the pistol at arm's length," said the conjuror.

Denis did as instructed.

"At my count of three, being certain the pistol is aimed point-blank at my face, pull the trigger. *One!*"

Sharp, asthmatic breathing punctuated the silence.

"*Two!*"

Diana noted the stiff line of Denis' jaw, the whiteness of his trigger finger, the distracted glare of his eye. Unable to control herself, she rushed forward.

"Denis, don't!"

Simultaneously, Cagliostro called, "*Three!*"

Diana whipped her head down as the pistol crashed and thundered. Then she heard a thin femi-

# THE DEVIL HAS FOUR FACES

nine cry and opened her eyes as the world crashed down in ruins.

"My God!" Mrs. Grosswin shrieked. "He shot the magician!"

Cagliostro stared at the group with slack-mouthed horror. His fingers fluttered at the lapels of his robe. As he groaned and tugged his purple gown open, Diana saw revealed the gleaming white front of his dress shirt beneath. A male voice called out sharply. Karl Strauss surged forward from his chair. Cagliostro capered a step backward, incredulously daubing at the blood which gleamed wetly on his shirt bosom.

"I'm shot," he gasped in a perplexed, choking voice. "I'm shot!"

"A doctor . . ." someone cried.

As if driven beyond reason by shock, Cagliostro turned and fled for the doorway. "Doctor," he groaned wildly over his shoulder. "Must find doctor. Must find doctor . . ." He vanished through the black velvet hangings, leaving a trail of red on the marble floor behind him.

Windows crashed open as the guests crowded forward. Diana, driven along with the group, caught a flash of brilliant light, heard the growl of a motor and then the savage whine of tires on concrete. A servant rushed breathlessly into the room. "I tried to stop him, Mr. Strauss! He knocked me down, then staggered into his car and drove off."

Karl Strauss scowled. "I hope the man is not wounded so severely that he cannot drive. In any case, I must call the police. Out of my way, please." He shouldered through the throng. Others in the group retreated from the room until only Diana and her fiancé remained.

Denis stood unmoving, the pistol in his hand.

He raised agonized eyes to Diana. "I didn't shoot him. You saw that."

Numbly she made a negative nod. "My eyes were closed. I was frightened, Denis."

"I wanted to kill him!" Denis protested. "Yet when you screamed, I jerked my hand up. I shot high, well over his head." His voice rose. "Diana, this is God's truth. I shot over his head." He halted, hurt by the lack of belief on her face. Again he shouted, "I tell you I shot high!"

Diana approached the rose-papered wall and studied it; then she swung around, calculating the positions of Denis and the magician. Once more, she studied the wallpaper. Denis had been standing several yards in front of a clear stretch of wall, flanked on one side by a doorway and on the other by tall windows. His target area was all of fifteen feet wide.

Not a single blemish or perforation could be seen on the unpatterned rose paper. Diana shuddered as the black draperies swayed in the wind. From a remote part of the house came the voice of Karl Strauss shouting into a telephone.

"If you shot high," Diana whispered in terror, "then where is the bullet hole? And why was he bleeding?"

Denis met her gaze in numb bewilderment.

One hour after the shooting, a chilly autumnal rain began to descend from the night sky. On the mostly deserted stretch of highway connecting the suburb of Briarwood with the city proper stood a white-painted roadside establishment whose green neon sign proclaimed it as Ned's Highway Eats. From behind the broad plate-glass window of the diner, Ned Teller surveyed the slippery highway. The restaurant's lone customer finished the last bite of hamburger, drained his coffee cup and strolled to the cash register. Ned Teller accepted a dollar bill, rang up the sale and presented the customer with his change.

"It's a miserable night for driving," the customer said, turning up his coat collar.

Teller agreed. "I aim to close up. Business will be nil. There's been a shortage of cars all evening, matter of fact." As the customer prepared to depart, Teller applied a scraper to the grease-stained grill as the first step in his nightly cleanup. The customer's startled exclamation made him turn about, and as he did so, a pair of headlights rocketed past on the highway. The snarl of the speeding car echoed behind the dwindling taillights.

"Blazes!" Teller exclaimed. "That damn fool must be pushing eighty. Didn't he see the sign?" He pointed to the far side of the highway where a metal warning marker could be dimly glimpsed. "Why, just up ahead is one of the worst curves in this part of the country. If you come on it too fast, dead in front of you is an embankment that—"

A distant crash arrested his words.

Exchanging a look of consternation with the customer, Teller grabbed a slicker from a coat tree and shouted toward the kitchen: "Maud! Maud, call the cops. There's a wreck down the highway. And snap it up." Half out the door, Teller called, "Come on, stranger. Somebody may need our help."

They raced through the rain for nearly half a mile. Where the road made a sharp bend around a hillside, the racing automobile had crashed straight forward through the guard rail and rolled down the embankment. As Teller and his companion plunged down the gully wall, flames shot up from the wrecked car and an agonized scream of human pain split the rainy air. Teller and the stranger worked to free the jammed door as the flames leaped higher. Inside the caved-in car, one bloody hand beat on the cracked window glass, then slid out of sight. The flames grew too intense, and Teller and his companion leaped back, slapping out embers on their clothing. Teller's face contorted into a mask of horror.

"Poor devil in there," he said. "Poor devil . . ."

# THE DEVIL HAS FOUR FACES

The stranger clutched his arm. "Up the hill. Quick!"

The two men scrambled to safety. Five minutes before the police arrived, flames reached the gas tank and the automobile blew up.

Thunderous knocking shook the entrance hall of the Strauss mansion in Briarwood an hour later. The servant who answered the summons grew alarmed at the sight of a police prowl car parked in the driveway, its blinker revolving through the rain. Under the dripping portico stood a blunt-jawed man wearing a fedora. The man stuck out his hand and flashed an identification card.

"Captain Brainard from homicide," he stated in a tough, clipped voice. "Is Mr. Karl Strauss at home?"

The servant cast an apprehensive look at a patrolman standing by the official car, a massive gun belt around his waist. "Right this way, sir," he murmured. Brainard stepped into the hallway. Unshaven and untidy, he still radiated a definite air of authority.

The servant led him to the library, where a fire crackled in the grate. Karl Strauss approached as the servant announced:

"This gentleman is Captain Brainard of the homicide department, sir."

The servant withdrew and closed the library doors. Karl Strauss said with a frown, "You are not the policeman with whom I spoke on the telephone earlier this evening."

Brainard shook his head sharply. "You called the local station. As I get the story, Mr. Strauss, you reported that a magician entertaining here tonight suffered a gunshot wound, left hastily while shouting for a doctor, and drove his car away." Brainard perched on the corner of a walnut desk and tilted back his hat, revealing grayed temples. He flipped open a small pad. "Please give me the magician's name, and describe his clothing."

Strauss locked his hands behind his back and peered into the dancing flames. "His contract, which I signed a day or two ago, specified his name as Richard Fuchs. He appeared professionally as Cagliostro the Magician. Tonight he wore . . . let's see . . . a purple gown, of silk, I think, decorated in gold with symbols of the zodiac. Beneath the robe . . . ah, yes! full evening clothes. I recall that detail because he tore the robe open and I saw blood on the front of his shirt."

Brainard made a series of rapid check marks on the page. "The name Fuchs fits with the registration of the car, and the description of the robe tallies with the fragment of unburned cloth we found in the wreckage."

"Wreckage?" echoed Strauss.

"That's correct," Brainard said. "Roughly one hour after leaving your house, Richard Fuchs had an accident on the city highway, about three miles from here. His car plunged down an embankment and burst into flames. The man's body was burned beyond recognition."

Strauss gasped softly. Brainard continued: "Again the local station was phoned, by a Mrs. Ned Teller. Another report has also come in from a physician in the neighborhood. The wounded man, apparently, turned up on the doctor's doorstep shortly after leaving here, begging for help. The doctor became frightened, hesitated, and Fuchs fled. Then the doctor made a report, to be on the safe side.

"While driving to the city to get help, Fuchs appears to have weakened and lost control. Anyway, the local station called City Homicide and I rushed out. Now . . ." Brainard's eyes flicked at the older man. "Who shot the magician?"

Karl Strauss frowned. "I assure you that the shooting was a complete accident."

"We'll see."

"The magician was shot by my niece's fiancé, Denis Blaine. Blaine and my niece Diana are still in the house."

Stalking to the door, Brainard said, "If you please, I'd like to speak with this man Blaine."

"Very well."

They found Denis Blaine and Diana in the kitchen, morosely sipping cups of lukewarm coffee. Denis listened with a wooden expression to Captain Brainard's explanation of his mission.

"Are you certain that Fuchs was the accident victim?" Denis asked in a thick voice.

"Reasonably certain," Brainard said. "We made an identification from the license plates. We dug out one scrap of purple cloth with gold thread upon it. And I'm told by the coroner's people that while Fuchs is terribly charred, the bullet in the man's body will be available for examination."

"There is a bullet in his body?" Denis said, stunned. "Captain, I did not shoot the man! I fired over his head at the last second. I—" Realizing that his words held no meaning when torn out of the context of the story, Denis began again: "When I tell you the truth about Fuchs, as he called himself, you'll understand."

"Perhaps," muttered Brainard. "I have a car in front. Let's go, Mr. Blaine." Thrusting his hands into the pockets of his tan raincoat, he left the kitchen. Karl Strauss followed. Diana hung back and gripped her fiancé's arm.

"Denis, this frightens me more every instant. I wonder whether telling the truth is the best course."

His laugh had a forced quality. "Darling, when I explain the whole mess, everything is bound to clear up. The only way out of this tangle is to reveal the whole truth. Wait until they check on Fuchs. His record will come into the open."

Diana murmured, "I only hope so."

Her last sight of Denis was as he stepped out beneath the rain-drenched portico. Brainard opened the door of the prowl car for him, slammed it, then sprinted around to the other side. The signal flasher spun to life and the car roared away down the drive.

At three-thirty that morning, in a cold, poorly lighted room at police headquarters, Denis Blaine was arrested for murder.

The Pacific Minerals Building in the center of the city provided the owning corporation with five floors of lavish office space, and with a substantial income from the eight additional floors, much less lavish, rented by persons who desired a "good" address. On the sixth floor of this building a single corridor ran straight back from the elevators, flanked by uninteresting and uniform rows of frosted glass doorways. Sandwiched between the Teafly Watch Spring Works and the Sacramento Decalcomania Company Sales Office was a doorway which bore a simple legend: M. P. SMITH; and below it, in smaller black lettering, INVESTIGATIONS.

Behind this door was a bare one-room office furnished with desk, typewriter, wastebasket, two chairs, filing cabinet, telephone, coat tree and—the only touch of luxury—Venetian blinds. Two days after the arrest of Denis Blaine, at nine-thirty on a crisp sunlit morning, Marco Polo Smith, after many false starts and innumerable cigarettes, attacked his battered Underwood.

Rolling a fresh sheet of paper into the platen,

and wincing at the thought of writing a report on the divorce investigation he had been conducting, he glanced wistfully at a thin volume lying on the scarred desk top. The book was a real treasure—a recently discovered memoir by Henry Knox, a Boston bookseller who had commanded an expedition during the winter of 1775-76 to freight captured cannon from Fort Ticonderoga to Cambridge, Massachusetts, thereby enabling General Washington to capture the city of Boston.

Marco loved history the way the alcoholic loves liquor. He had been named by a schoolteacher father who revered Marco Polo as a symbol of an individualism which the father believed dying at the time his only son was born. Through a rambling combination of circumstances, Marco P. Smith—often called by his friends Military Police Smith, or Member of Parliament Smith—had entered the detective agency business and done rather well.

He typed away, a tallish, slender young man—well over six feet when standing—with sandy hair and a face that could only be described as pleasantly ugly. Marco cared little for modern contrivances, but in his desk drawer could be found a .38 revolver of the most advanced design, in a specially engineered holster. He customarily wore rather conservative glen plaid suits, and wool ties of a solid color, but beyond these characteristics, he was undistinguished in appearance. Only a close

# THE DEVIL HAS FOUR FACES

inspection would reveal a slightly cauliflowered left ear, remnant of a promising ring career.

At the squeaky sound of the doorknob's turn, he rose with immeasurable relief. The door opened. His visitor was a copper-haired girl in a lime wool-knit dress and a dark coat.

"Are you Mr. Marco Smith, the detective?"

"That's right."

She closed the door and advanced toward the desk. Marco noticed the weary lines and shadows on her face as she said:

"My name is Diana Meadows, Mr. Smith. I need your help urgently."

## CHAPTER IV

Denis paced the gloomy cell in City Prison with angry steps. A chill hung over the grim, harshly lighted cubicle, matched by a bleak autumn-gray sky beyond the small window up near the ceiling.

Marco Smith perched on the edge of the bunk, toying with his hat, while Denis repeated the story of his imprisonment in Berlin, including the death of Quigley and the events at the home of Karl Strauss leading to his arrest. At the finish, Marco gave a slight, meaningless nod.

"That is substantially the story Miss Meadows told me yesterday. Frankly, Blaine, I never like operating counter to the police. But in this instance —well, your story has such a wild ring that it hooked me from the start."

Denis turned an agonized face to the detective, his hands wide, pleading.

"Until I walked into police headquarters I believed in the virtue of truth. Thirty minutes after I told my story to the police, they arrested me.

# THE DEVIL HAS FOUR FACES

Brainard laughed when I suggested that Fuchs, or Cagliostro, or whatever his name was, might be a Nazi general living out a new identity." Denis raked a hand through his rumpled hair. "I belted a couple of cops." Denis did not see Marco's mild smile as he went on: "In the opinion of the police —and I understand now the district attorney concurs—I made a faulty identification and killed a perfectly responsible, loyal American citizen."

Marco's eyes flicked with interest. "Fuchs had identification?"

"Brainard says it turned up, yes."

"Money can buy almost anything," Marco said thoughtfully. "Even a new identity for a Nazi. Did you point out that an investigation could be made to check for forged papers?"

Denis nodded bitterly. "But all the guilty actions seem to be on my side. I saw the magician's flyer at the dinner table. I lost my head." He raised his hands again to signify inevitability. "I shot an innocent man."

"Yet you told me the magician confessed that he was your General Fuchs-Ohm, when you talked to him in the kitchen before the performance."

"Who the hell can corroborate that?" Denis shot back.

Catching the other man's mood of unrest, Marco lit a cigarette and walked toward the bars. "The medical examination produced the bullet from the charred body of the man who died in the accident."

Marco swung around. "The bullet was marked with a six-pointed star—three intersecting straight lines. And two dozen witnesses saw you scratch that sign on a bullet at the party."

Denis stared stonily toward the gray-backed pane of glass. "It's not necessary to repeat all the grim details, Smith."

"You swear you shot high at the last second?"

"Yes." Denis smashed his fist against the bunk. "Damn it, yes!"

"The wall was unmarked."

"I can't help that. I shot high."

"Fuchs began to bleed right after the shot was fired."

Whipping to his feet, Denis faced the detective. "Are you on my side or not? If you don't care to be bothered by the whole mess, send the retainer check back to Diana and go to hell!"

Silence.

Marco Polo Smith showed no anger, no alarm. Denis sighed.

"I'm sorry." He sank down on the bunk. "But do you understand how it feels to keep thinking—"

"Certainly," Marco replied smoothly. "In a climate where political expediency demands the quick, unsubtle answer, a fast trial and faster punishment, you're in a rough spot. Had you shot a man who, say, attacked your fiancée two weeks ago, you would go free. But the origins of this case are buried in a war whose horrors most people have forgotten. And to make matters worse, we're bedeviled with tricks . . ."

"Tricks?" echoed Denis.

"Sure," Marco replied swiftly. "The bullet-catching illusion, for instance. Normally, when the stunt is performed and the pistol fired, there would be no bullet in the muzzle."

"You know how the trick works?" Denis asked.

"Time for that later. What puzzles me now is the fact that you must have shot a bullet at the wall, over the magician's head, but that same bullet appears to have taken a left turn in the air and buried itself in the victim's belly. The magician then went looking for medical help, turned up on the doorstep of this—this Dr. Charles Massilon. The doctor grew frightened. The magician went away. But not before the doctor saw clearly that the magician's shirt was heavily stained with blood. Finally Fuchs —or Fuchs-Ohm—climbed into his car and drove toward the city. Wrecked the car. And was burned to a crisp."

Marco revolved the brim of his hat between his fingers.

"It all falls neatly into place, except for three things." He threw the hat aside and looked at Denis. "The interesting matter of the left-turn bullet. What it means I can't say, but it strikes me wrong. Second, the long time lapse between the magician's departure from the Strauss mansion and his wreck on the highway. Counting perhaps five minutes spent on Dr. Massilon's doorstep, what did the magician do for the remaining forty or fifty minutes? His car was piled up only about three miles from the Strauss home. And third . . ." Marco's eyes narrowed. "I can't escape the very interesting speculation that the magician might have been the Nazi general after all. If that could be proved, you would certainly go free."

Marco watched the prisoner carefully for a sign of reaction. Denis merely shook his head. "I have actually come to wonder whether the man was Fuchs-Ohm after all. Perhaps I was wrong." He turned empty, frightened eyes toward the detective. "Perhaps I really do belong in the gas chamber."

Marco picked up his hat. "No, somehow I can't bring myself to believe it." He held out his hand. "Thanks for your co-operation."

"You haven't promised me freedom," Denis said sardonically.

Marco shot him a level gaze. "If I did that, I would be a fool."

At the reception cubicle, Marco retrieved his valuables, wallet and belt, and as he was buckling the latter into place, a steel door opened and Diana Meadows entered. She rushed forward anxiously.

"Can you help . . . ?"

The detective shook his head. "Too early for an opinion. Can I get into the Strauss home tonight?"

"Yes. Here, take this." Diana fumbled in her bag, produced a key. "I alerted the servants. Uncle Karl will be away at a meeting, so you'll have free run of the place. Cousin Andrew may be home, but if you explain to him, he'll understand." She cast worried eyes toward the steel portal which led into the cell block. "Keep in touch with me, Mr. Smith, please. Everything depends on you."

Leaving the building, Marco encountered Captain Brainard. The police officer grinned from under the brim of his fedora.

"Hello, Smith. I heard you had been suckered into the Blaine business."

Marco respected Brainard's thoroughness but disliked his stubbornness in fastening on a single idea as the truth. "Does that irritate you, Captain?"

"Not a bit. Blaine just made a mistake, shot the wrong man. This Nazi claptrap may be true enough —I mean, the Berlin portion—but Fuchs was certainly no Hitler aide in disguise. He even has an Army record in Washington, and a birth certificate from Cincinnati, Ohio. Don't think we didn't check."

"The right amount of money can purchase anything," Marco replied. "Even insertion of a phony record in Washington. Or the name and papers of a man who died in battle. It might pay to do some additional investigation."

"Exactly how?" Brainard snapped. "How would you propose to prove the dead man was a Nazi general, instead of the person all trustworthy identification states him to be?"

"I have no idea," Marco admitted.

Brainard uttered a short laugh. "Then you had better take what money you can get from Blaine's friends. When he steps into the gas chamber—as he will soon—your chances will be gone. Denis Blaine shot an innocent man in cold blood. And he's going to pay."

Brainard passed into the building, and Marco Polo Smith descended the wind-swept steps of city prison.


Harry Soames parked his battered coupé in front of Ned's Highway Eats. He had just driven past the site of the accident and surveyed the wrecked railing. He carried a letter which had arrived in his mailbox that morning and was already worn from nervous handling. Slipping onto a stool at the deserted counter, he noticed that a large wall clock advertising Coca-Cola showed the time as a quarter past eight. He would allow himself fifteen minutes before keeping his appointment, and eat a bite of dinner in the meantime—his first reason for stopping at this particular spot.

Harry Soames resembled a weasel come to human life. Sunken cheeks narrowed down to a delicate pointed chin, and all his features appeared to have been squeezed forcibly into the limits of his face. Rather seedily dressed, he maintained a hangdog expression which made him somehow likable in spite of his pitiable and suspicious appearance.

# THE DEVIL HAS FOUR FACES 59

Teller approached, wiping his hands on his apron. "Yours?"

"Number four," Soames stammered, glancing up from the menu. "Pork chop, apple sauce. And a cup of coffee. With cream, please." As Teller turned his back and relayed the order to the kitchen, Soames' hand stole across the counter. He grasped the salt cellar and slipped it into the pocket of his overcoat. When Teller faced front again, Soames was staring at the menu. Teller threw him a queer look and strolled away.

The next few minutes became an agonizing experience for Harry Soames. Did he dare question the man? Teller brought the meal, and while he was drawing a cup of coffee from a shining urn, Soames fished from his wallet an old identification card he had used before the state revoked his private detective's license.

"See here a second . . . I'm an investigator," Soames muttered vaguely. "Are you Teller, the man who found the body of the magician the other night?"

"Correct," Teller answered, trying to get a clearer look at the identification which Soames returned to his pocket in haste. "I thought I had about answered all the questions on the subject." Teller shuddered involuntarily. "I never will forget the sight of that burned, blackened—"

"Please!" Soames protested, attempting to eat a spoonful of applesauce. "I wanted to find out whether the police turned up any identification at the scene of the wreck other than what the paper listed. Anything besides the scrap of purple cloth with gold markings."

"Not while I was on the scene," Teller declared emphatically. "And I hung around until the ambulance hauled the body away and the police wrecker came for the car." Teller hunched forward, elbows on the counter. "What's your angle on the case, mister? You say you're a private detective?"

"That's right." Soames averted his eyes. "But I can't reveal anything about my client. You understand, Mr. Teller—professional ethics and all that."

"Oh," Teller replied, "I see." He walked away.

Soames attacked his food again, but abandoned the effort after a few mouthfuls, too upset to risk any greater load on his stomach. Rising to pay the check, his hand crept out and seized the pepper shaker. With the article half-pocketed, he turned beet-red when Teller exclaimed loudly:

"Hey, mister! What's the idea trying to swipe the pepper?"

Soames stammered a confused apology, drew out the salt shaker also and replaced both on the counter. Teller sputtered in surprise. Soames fled out the door. He squealed the auto's tires and careened onto the highway without looking back. His face crawled with clammy, unwholesome sweat.

Like an automaton, he maneuvered the turns and curves of the road which led toward the Strauss mansion in Briarwood. His pitiful effort to get information from Teller had been a total flop. Teller only substantiated the account Soames had read with horror in the daily newspapers. Fresh beads of sweat popped out on his forehead and trickled down alongside his nose, even though the evening had turned chilly. The warm yellow lights glowing behind the windows of Briarwood mansions only heightened his despair.

Harry Soames hated his hands.

They had cost him his detective's license. A psychiatrist had once told him that kleptomania was rooted in the brain, the result of a mental quirk. Yet Soames had never been able to free himself from the notion that his hands had a terrible malignant personality all their own. They almost seemed to act separately from his mind, landing him time and again into trouble.

At the end of one particularly bleak spell of unemployment, when he barely managed to stay alive, he had made his alliance with the magician and taken up the business of blackmail. And while he was fairly well paid, he hated his task, felt that the world had driven him to a criminal's life. Usually he disliked making a collection, but tonight he dreaded it even more, because of the letter which rested like a burning coal in the pocket of his cheap overcoat.

Soames recognized the iron grille marking the entrance to the Strauss mansion. He turned his coupé up the drive, parked in the shadows a good distance from the portico, and got out. A bitter autumn wind soughed the pines around the front of the house. Soames saw only one light in the entire place, gleaming far back behind a curtained window. With trepidation in his soul, Harry Soames thumbed the bell and heard it clang in the remote regions of the house.

The wind keened through the boughs, making an eerie sound. No one came to answer the doorbell. Halfway out from under the portico, he said to himself, I can run, hop a flight to California or some other spot. He could never find me, even if—

Behind him, the door opened.

"Oh," said Soames, climbing the steps again. "I thought no one was home."

"I am here," replied Andrew Strauss, a motionless figure in the shadows. "Come in, Mr. Soames."

Soames approached the door. "Would you walk ahead of me, please?"

He did not like Andrew's chuckle. Following the millionaire into the house, he disliked even more the sound of their footsteps clacking in the high, dark foyer. A suit of armor on a pedestal loomed up on his right like some evil god. Soames hurried behind the other man toward the open double doors through which firelight flickered.

Andrew Strauss moved aside while Soames stepped into the library. Then Andrew closed the doors and rubbed his hands together. His eyes had a bright quality and his face a flushed color which Soames marked as signs of some sort of weird humor. Soames inhaled the aromas of burning wood and leather book bindings, shifting his feet nervously on the carpet.

"Care for a drink?" Andrew inquired, falsely polite.

"No, thanks," Soames answered.

"How about taking off your coat before we get down to business? It's very close in here."

"Never mind." Soames jockeyed for a position before the fireplace. Directly behind his head hung a large mirror, which added an illusion of gloomy depth to the room. He wished urgently that he had brought a pistol along. Each time before when he had made the collection, Andrew Strauss had seemed angry and belligerent. Tonight he appeared just the opposite.

"No need to prolong the agony," Soames began with a flimsy smile. "If you will just get the cash for me . . ."

"I do not have the money," Andrew said slowly.

Soames blinked. "Now, wait a second. If you don't pay, there will be trouble."

"Is that a fact?" Andrew breathed. His eyes appeared suddenly heavy and puffed. He stepped forward. "We are alone in this house, Soames. And before you leave, I intend that you tell me the name of the man who employs you. The man"—Andrew's voice hardened as he dealt out the words—"who knows so much about my transactions at a certain bank in Buenos Aires."

"I can't do that," Soames argued, frightened. "I might be killed myself."

"Nevertheless, you will tell me," Andrew repeated. His face went ugly, blotched with anger.

"Hold it!" Soames protested, his voice rising to a pitch of reedy fright. "If you're going to get rough, let me out of—"

"I am going to kill you," Andrew Strauss shouted hoarsely, "unless you tell me his name!"

Soames broke suddenly for the door, tripped over a chair and reeled back against the fireplace, narrowly missing the flames. With a bellow of rage, Andrew Strauss caught up a pair of iron fire tongs from the hearth.

"Tell me his name!" he roared. "Tell me!"

Andrew clasped both hands on the tongs and brought them around at shoulder level in a murderously powerful arc. Crying out, Soames ducked. The tongs shattered the mirror.

"Tell me his name!" Andrew screamed.

Soames attempted to duck again. The tongs connected with his skull in a glancing blow. Half-unconscious, he slumped to the floor and awaited the final stroke that would bring death. Dazedly, he heard a crashing of wood, hoarse oaths, a second voice shouting words he could not decipher. Then his fear plunged him into unconsciousness.

# CHAPTER V

When Marco Smith pulled his convertible into the driveway of the Strauss mansion, he noted the ramshackle coupé half visible in the windy shadows on the far side of the portico. Unbending his lanky frame from beneath the wheel of his own car, Smith padded forward, slipped a pencil flash from his breast pocket and shone the tiny beam on the registration case strapped to the steering column. He noted the name of the owner—Harry Soames—and memorized the address, filing it in his memory. A faint frown wrinkled his brow. He snapped out the flash and walked back to the portico.

Carefully, he thumbed the handle. The door moved silently open.

He entered the darkened hall. A hoarse cry, then a tremendous crashing of glass burst through the house, followed by the repeated roar of a man's voice.

Marco raced toward the source of the shouting. One lifted foot kicked the library door open with a bang. He hung on the doorframe a second while his mind focused the scene. Then he leaped forward to rip a pair of bloodied fire tongs from the hands of Andrew Strauss.

Andrew cursed, his eyes rolling wildly as he wrestled with his new adversary. Marco hurled the tongs across the floor with a clang.

"Out of the way!" Andrew howled, butting his head against Marco, who stood as the only barrier between him and his groaning victim lying near the hearth.

"Back," Marco warned with a push. "Back, sweetheart." His lips quirked as he cocked a fist and unrolled a punch which rocketed Andrew across the library and threw him into a skidding easy chair, where he collapsed in a heap. Slouched down on the base of his spine, glaring at Marco out of fat eyelids, he breathed fitfully and prepared to rise.

Marco said nothing. He hefted the fire tongs, raised them across his chest and waited.

A log in the grate broke, fell and shot up a shower of hissing orange sparks. The tiny motes of fire reflected in the shards of broken mirror scattered on the hearth. For a moment, miniature points of orange light danced across the ceiling. The stiffness left Andrew Strauss' frame. Marco replaced the tongs in the holder with a clank, then bent over the prostrate victim.

Harry Soames sat upright with Marco's assistance.

# THE DEVIL HAS FOUR FACES

He dabbed experimentally at his forehead and his fingers came away slightly reddened.

"My God," he exclaimed, struggling. "I'm going to die."

Marco smiled. "Pull yourself together. You're Harry Soames, aren't you? Licensed investigator once, if I remember."

Soames nodded. "And I recognize your face. Marco Polo Smith. How can I thank you? He would have bashed my brains out."

Marco helped Soames to his feet and pointed him toward the door. "If you have no objections, I'll prescribe the best medicine for the situation—a fast exit." He added a final shove toward the hallway. "Your head doesn't look too badly cut. I'd drop in at a drugstore, and if you feel yourself getting sleepy, telephone a doctor."

Soames pumped Marco's hand with frantic gratitude, and proceeded into the gloom of the hall. The outside door closed softly. Marco swung around to confront the brooding man still slumped where the detective had shoved him. Marco cocked his fists on his hips.

"You," he said sharply, "I should turn over to the cops."

"What the hell makes it your affair?" Andrew said.

Marco put a cigarette in one corner of his mouth and squinted through the flame of his match.

"Andrew Strauss, correct?" Marco flipped the match deftly into the fire.

Andrew leaned forward, tiredly belligerent. "That sniveling little—who just left here said your name was Smith? Speaking of the police, what business do you have in this house? I have half a mind to have you arrested."

Marco drew out a key. "On what charge?"

"What's that? A key to this house? Where did you get it?"

"From Diana Meadows."

"From Diana—!" Andrew sputtered. "Has she taken to passing them around to every bum she meets?" Andrew sniggered unpleasantly. He hoisted himself to his feet and tottered in the direction of a built-in cabinet bar. He jolted three fingers of bourbon into a glass and swallowed it like medicine. Marco studied him, sensing the man's bravado as a kind of last-ditch bastion thrown up hastily to wall himself off from the turmoil obviously seething in his mind.

In six sentences, Marco explained the purpose of his visit.

"Denis blew a hole in the magician, all right," Andrew muttered, already on his second drink. "I viewed the whole stupid scene." Bravado had melted into a maudlin thickening of his tongue. "You think Denis Blaine needs to worry? You think he's in a bad spot?" Andrew threw back his head

# THE DEVIL HAS FOUR FACES

and laughed. Then he poured himself another drink.

"I trust you won't bother me if I go ahead with my examination of the music room," Marco said, ambling toward the door. Andrew Strauss merely snuffled. Marco did not turn around, but he heard a gurgle of liquid.

Ten minutes in the rose-papered music room with the somber black draperies convinced Marco that the damning evidence against Denis Blaine was without flaw—like the wallpaper where a bullet hole would have been, if Denis had truly fired over the head of Cagliostro the Magician. Marco extinguished the lights and prepared to leave. Passing the open library, his curiosity drew him to glance in at Andrew Strauss. The beer heir's stout frame was slumped into a doughy pile at his desk.

Marco stood in the door. Andrew had overturned a drink on the desk top. In its slopped remains he traced a symbol with his index finger, while Marco watched.

Marco craned forward. Abruptly he felt a cold wind sweep across his mind.

The fat finger of Andrew Strauss drew the design of a swastika.

Marco pulled a chair up beside the desk. Half-intoxicated, Andrew Strauss regarded him blearily.

"I wanted to kill that rotten little worm," Andrew wheezed. "I'm sick of bleeding to death in slow stages. You should tell Denis that plenty others

... other ... people have big troubles. Troubles that eat the soul, Mr. Whatever-your-name-is." Again Andrew Strauss sniggered. Then his face collapsed into exaggerated sorrow. "All because of one silly mistake," he muttered.

Marco hardly dared breathe. His heart raced like a hound on the scent of blood. "Why do you keep tracing that swastika?" he asked softly.

"Do you think I would tell you?" Andrew asked craftily.

"Won't you?"

Dumb indecision flickered in the stout man's eyes. Then he shook his head and babbled, "German origins, you understand. American citizen, father naturalized soon as he could off the boat. Raised right, y'see. But when war came, I told him I felt I should help the homeland. Wrong idea. I was mixed up. He argued, fought me. I was younger, crazy, but I scraped thirty thousand dollars together in forty-two, through contacts. Deposited in a bank in Argentina. The money went to help the war effort of the fatherland. All very secret. Only ..." Andrew Strauss sucked in his breath and faced his fear. ". . . Only someone knows. That little so-and-so comes here to drain me."

"Blackmail?"

Strauss blinked, his only sign of affirmation. "Can't you understand?" he whined. "I was foolish, idealistic. Thirty days after I sent the money, I knew it was wrong. Others donated, American-Germans, not many, but a few. What if my name ever got out? Father believes I never sent the money. Yet someone knows. Terrible part is that the only persons who could know were the ones who finally received the money. Someone from Germany, perhaps from the High Command. Because Soames showed me a photostat of a page from a book written in German. The donation was recorded on that page. Oh, what a miserable mess . . ."

Andrew pitched forward on his arm, burying his face, weeping. When he fell into the spilled liquor the pool widened and began to drip steadily off the desk at one spot. Marco rose slowly.

"Perhaps," he repeated, "from the High Command?"

At the sound of his voice, Andrew whipped his head up. A stupid sideways smile of cunning warped his mouth. "Think you know so much? Think I spilled everything? Confession's therapeutic. Ver . . . ver . . ." He stumbled over the simple word, and then repeated, "Therapeutic. I'll deny. Say anything and I'll deny, deny, deny. Kill you if you ask for money. Like killing that little weasel blackmailer if he comes around again." Andrew lowered his voice persuasively. "What did I tell you? What have I been babbling?"

Marco took a step to the rear. "Nothing. Relax."

Scuttling around the desk, Andrew bent himself into a near-cringing posture. "How much did I say?"

Marco spun and stalked through the hallway. He felt exhilarated, plunging into a strange new byway of intrigue. From the library, just as he closed the front door, a voice wailed: "Deny it! Deny every word! Never told you—"

Marco crashed the door closed and ran for his car, his coat flapping.


"The truth."

Marco Smith spoke the words and nailed Harry Soames with a demanding look.

Soames bit his lip; his shifty gaze switched to the illuminated pinball table. He shot the plunger and watched the steel ball rebound off a series of bumpers. Bells rang and lights of different hues flickered on the gaudy back panel. The steady crash-crash-crash of a rifle came from the arcade's shooting gallery. Three khaki-clad soldiers reeled through the door and shoved by on their way to the picture-viewers in the dim rear room.

Deliberately, Soames fired his last ball up the runway. Marco reached out and shook the game box. On the rear panel a tiny purple sign lit up—*Tilt*.

"Why did you do that?" Soames protested.

"Because I've put in nearly twenty-four hours tracking you down," Marco replied pleasantly. He drew cigarettes from his tan raincoat. Soames refused the offer with a rabbit shake of his head.

# THE DEVIL HAS FOUR FACES

Marco lit up. "Finally I located you here." He sniffed the penny-arcade aroma compounded of peanuts and the cashier's brilliantine. "This your office?"

Soames shifted. "Sort of. Smith, I can't afford an inch of trouble. I have a devil of a time just keeping alive. Why, whenever I walk into a store I risk catching a slice of big time." Unhappily he examined his pale hands, then thrust them into his pockets. "It's pure hell when you have a pair of hands that pick up anything in sight, no matter what your mind tells 'em to do."

Marco nodded. "But last night you nearly wrote period to it all. I thought you appreciated my keeping Strauss from bashing your brains in."

"Well, cripes, I did, but—"

Marco cut him off: "All I want is the truth, short and very sweet. Half a dozen elementary answers." Marco leaned forward insistently. "Come on, sweetheart. This is M. P. Smith talking. Your benefactor. Why are you blackmailing Strauss?"

"Were!"

"What?"

"'Were' is the word. I'm finished. Even if I starve, I never will make another try on that bozo Strauss. Almost falling into a coffin once is enough."

"Give me the answers before I get sore," Marco said softly.

Throwing a nervous glance at the street entrance, Soames bit his lip again. His eyes fixed in rigid concentration upon the pinball board. Marco let him set his own pace, sensing his readiness as well as his gripping fear. Soames clutched the sides of the pinball case with hands that were white and thin. In a remote voice, he began to speak to his face, reflected obliquely in the glass covering the illuminated board.

"I worked for a guy who came in here one night. He knew all about me. Lost license, everything. He was also aware that I needed dough in the worst way. He described the routine. I would contact Strauss, and say that his thirty-thousand-dollar deposit with the International Bank in Buenos Aires would be public information unless he forked over three hundred a week. I called every two weeks, and after a month and a half the ante jacked to five hundred per."

"Who hired you?"

Only after Soames spoke his next words did Marco begin to understand the look of panic in the ex-detective's ferret eyes. "His name was Richard Fuchs. A professional magician. He had a little room, or shop, in the Pomfret Building. Sometimes I met him there to pass over the money."

"You took a cut?"

"Hundred-and-fifty every second week."

"Strauss mentioned a photostat of a page from a book written in German. Did Fuchs give it to you?"

"Yes. He took it back after I showed it to Strauss."

"Did you ever try to quit on him?"

"A couple of times. Strauss grew tougher to handle with every collection. But Fuchs said he would kill me if I chickened." Soames darted Marco a glance of terror. "He had eyes with nothing behind them, that man. Pure emptiness. I felt pinned to the wall when he gave me a stare. I knew he meant what he said."

"Did you understand the reference to Buenos Aires?"

"No. Fuchs warned me never to get nosy. But Strauss evidently caught the meaning okay."

"Why are you so frightened, Harry? Richard Fuchs is dead. His car crashed out near Briarwood several days ago. An hour after his performance at the Strauss mansion."

In a hollow voice, Soames said, "I know the papers said it that way."

Marco's eyes narrowed. "Do you know something the papers didn't tell?"

"Yes." The same craftiness which had clouded the expression of Andrew Strauss now crept into the face of the ex-detective. "My cards are on the table, Smith. You saved my neck and I owe you a favor. What I told you is between the two of us. If you get any notions about singing to the police, forget them. I'll clam so fast they couldn't pry my mouth open with a crowbar. This mess scares me to death, and I figure on staying alive. Clear?" He had acquired a singular degree of resoluteness while he spoke.

Marco shook his head. "No. Not at all."

Soames glowered. "Then read this." From an inner pocket he produced an envelope containing a typewritten letter. Marco unfolded the paper and read it:

REGARDLESS OF WHAT YOU READ IN THE PAPERS, CONTINUE YOUR COLLECTIONS. PLACE THE CASH IN AN ENVELOPE AND DROP IT THROUGH THE MAIL SLOT OF THE SHOP IN THE POMFRET BUILDING. FAIL TO CARRY THIS OUT AND YOUR LIFE WILL BE WORTH NOTHING. FUCHS.

Crash-crash-crash exploded the rifles at the shooting gallery. One of the soldiers uttered a drunken, hysterical laugh.

Marco refolded the sheet and returned it to the envelope. "Postmarked well after Fuchs had his wreck. When did you receive it?"

"Yesterday morning. I—I picked up my mail at the Atlas Bar and Grill down the street. Fuchs knew the address." Soames' eyes widened and he whispered feverishly, "But Fuchs is supposed to be dead. Did he come back, Smith? Did he get up out of the morgue and start walking around again?"

Marco placed a hand on the ex-detective's trembling arm. "Take it easy. Have you received any other messages? Any telephone calls?"

Soames waved the letter. "Isn't this bad enough?"

Marco nodded. He indicated to Soames that he was ready to leave. The two men went out into a mist-shrouded street. Street lights gleamed distantly and the air smelled heavy with autumn's decay. Marco turned up the collar of his coat. Soames blinked fearfully in the wash of pink light falling from the arcade's neon sign.

"All I want to do is crawl into a hole and hide until someone makes sense out of this," Soames breathed. "I—I really do appreciate how you saved my skin last night, Smith. That's why I spilled. And if you ever land in a spot where you might need a leg man, sort of off the record, without a license and all, I sure could use the cash. I know you won't run to the police." Then he blinked. "Will you?"

"You told me you wouldn't talk if I did."

"I could still catch a blackmail rap . . ."

Marco shook his head. "Move along, Harry. Find a place to buy a good stiff drink and calm your nerves. If I need help, I'll call."

Soames muttered a few disjointed syllables and set out down the block. Marco watched him disappear through the mist, a bent, beaten, strangely likable man, caught in the grip of powers beyond his comprehension. Marco figured that Soames had already paid triple for serving as a blackmail tool. The ravages of fright were adding a month to the ex-detective's age every minute.

Marco returned to his car and headed through the gathering mist toward the Pomfret Building.

A five spot gained him entrance past the garrulous octogenarian who served as building guard. Marco studied the lobby directory by light of the custodian's large flash. Fuchs, R. rented office space on the fourth floor. Since the elevator was not running, Marco took the stairs. He climbed and the shadows closed around him, thick, echoing with the ghostly sounds of his own footfalls. His nerves beat a sharp little tattoo along his pulse as he emerged on the fourth-floor corridor. Down past a small service light the corridor was swallowed by black. Marco walked softly.

The Black Arts Shop had a frosted glass door. Marco paused outside, extracting a set of keys from his pocket. His eyes concentrated on a tiny spot of illumination glowing through the glass from the opposite side. Someone was working by a nearly concealed light. Marco's hands worked swiftly, until the third key turned. The lock scratched faintly. Replacing the key, Marco took out his .38 and turned the doorknob.

By the time the door swung all the way open the telltale light had blinked out.

By the dim reflections of the hall service bulb Marco could make out the general features of the

# THE DEVIL HAS FOUR FACES

shop. He stepped to the side of the doorway, waiting. A clock ticked. Then came the scuff of a foot moving on the hardwood floor. Marco advanced toward a showcase. Apparatus gleamed faintly behind glass. Marco crouched down.

The shoe-scuff whispered again. Marco looked left, then right. Over his right shoulder towered a massive glass case which housed the painted statue of a gypsy woman wearing a turban. Her plaster of Paris hands were raised in supplication, palms upward; her eyeballs gleamed whitely blank as she stared sightlessly into the future, a horrible apparition rising up in the gloom.

The footsteps made a sudden scurry.

Marco started to rise, heard a creaking sound, and whipped his head around.

The glass fortune-telling case teetered forward; the blind gypsy loomed over him. Marco cried out sharply, and tried to dodge.

The case crashed down on him with all its massive weight. The glass shattered, the gypsy fell in large pieces, and Marco collapsed beneath the wreckage, half-conscious. He was pinned. After a moment his mind was driven senseless by the shock of the blow.

A stealthy figure crawled over the wreckage of the gypsy case. From beneath a counter a hand drew forth a large tin of cleaning fluid. The liquid sloshed in the can as the dark figure sprinkled it across the floor. A match hissed, then the goods in the case caught fire. The dark figure closed the door and retreated into the hall. Under the fallen gypsy, the unconscious detective in the raincoat did not stir.

Moments later the fire escape door at the end of the corridor clanged open.

In The Black Arts Shop the flames danced higher. The smashed head of the gypsy began to smoke and burn.

Searing heat roasted Marco Smith's back. He opened his eyes and twisted his shoulders, spilling shards of the broken case onto the floor. Three feet away the gypsy's shattered head burned.

He attempted to rise, barely able to hoist his back beneath the burden of the fallen statue. His brain hummed, wavered in and out of unconsciousness. The hem of his raincoat caught fire and flared up. He lifted the mechanical figure, a ruin of gears, springs and flywheels, by tremendous exertion of his protesting arm muscles. He barely had time to slide from under the weight before his arms gave out and the statue crashed down. Only partially conscious, Marco stumbled to his feet and staggered past the burning showcase. Dimly the closed glass door loomed. Arms over his head, he butted through, smashing the frosted pane, spilling face first into the corridor beyond.

Ragged pain tore his legs. He glanced down,

# THE DEVIL HAS FOUR FACES

wrestled his burning coat like a living thing, finally managing to fling it away. Then he plunged on down the hall, away from the holocaust of black smoke boiling through the doorway of the blazing shop. An ache at the base of his skull became insistent, brutal, and his legs jellied under him. He rolled onto the floor. Cool marble pressed his cheek and he closed his eyes. The noise receded. The last bright splinter of dancing fire guttered and went dark.

Captain Brainard raised his voice on the opposite side of the hospital screen: "Madame, this is my police identification. Your patient asked to see me."

The fussy, gray-haired nurse became flustered. "But I have orders—"

Orders for what, Marco never learned. Brainard blustered around the screen and the hapless nurse retreated in confusion.

Marco put down the book he had been reading: a life of Peter Mark Roget, the amazing Londoner who had been, by turns, professor of medicine at the Manchester Infirmary, scientific researcher on the problems of consumption and nitrous oxide, consulting physician to Queen Charlotte's Lying-In Hospital, consultant to the government on London's water supply, adviser of Jeremy Bentham on disposal of London's sewage, editor of an important medical publication, inventor of a slide rule, a balance and a calculating machine, author of tomes on plant physiology, electricity and phrenology, contributor to encyclopedias and solver of complicated chess problems—all in addition to his massive fifty-year compilation of synonyms, antonyms, idioms, metaphors, phrases, similes, colloquialisms, foreign expressions and quotations, published in 1852 to the eternal benefit of those who fumble after words. Abandoning this colossus of learning, Marco turned his attention to the somewhat smaller colossus of official power waiting at his bedside.

Brainard perched on a corner of the covers in a slant of barred sunlight which fell through Venetian blinds into the clean, antiseptically sharp air of the room. Swathed in a white hospital gown and propped against a pillow, Marco half-grinned at the officer.

Brainard rolled a thin brown cigar between his fingers, then inserted it between his lips at a defiant angle. He said in slightly caustic tones: "Being ordered around by private detectives is not exactly a usual part of my routine."

"Ordered?" Marco arched his eyebrows. "Requested politely would be the right description."

"Were you burned badly?"

"Luckily, no. The doctor said I would be released after he changed the dressings this afternoon. Henceforth I shall pay my property taxes with exceeding joy, since they apparently finance the excellent fire department whose rescue squad rushed me here last night in a state of mental blankness, after

# THE DEVIL HAS FOUR FACES

the watchman of the Pomfret Building found me kayoed in the hall outside Fuchs' shop."

"That is a coincidence," Brainard said. "A fire in the magician's headquarters. You didn't by some wild chance call me here to explain, did you? That would be a stroke of luck I don't deserve."

Marco looked grieved. "I wanted you to be the first to know." He hunched forward amid the crisp sheets, a serious expression darkening his face. "I broke into the shop last night because I think Richard Fuchs is still alive. Someone was working in the shop when I got there—I saw a light. Fuchs pushed a mammoth fortune-telling case down on my head, then set fire to the furnishings, hoping to put a final period at the end of his trail."

Brainard leaped to his feet. "Fuchs?" he cried. "Man, your mind *has* left the track."

Marco grinned savagely. "You think so?"

Quickly he briefed the police captain with an account of the events which followed Diana's presentation of the key to the Strauss mansion. Marco did not omit his conversation with Andrew Strauss, nor the confessions made to him by the ex-detective, Harry Soames. Throughout the recital, Brainard's mood wavered visibly between disbelief and conviction, with the latter holding sway when Marco had finished.

"Blackmail, then?" Brainard repeated tightly. "I think we had better drag in Mr. Harry Soames for a little talk."

"You won't be able to prove blackmail," Marco warned.

"Why not?"

"Like Strauss and Soames, I'll deny every word. After all, Captain, Soames did me a favor. And he's suffered the tortures of hell already."

"Just because of one letter supposedly mailed by Fuchs after his death?"

"Right. Don't you realize there are bigger fish afloat than Soames? Besides, Strauss would refuse to admit a word of the story, unless you beat it from him. And I know your methods haven't become that depraved." Marco had scored a hit. Brainard flushed uncomfortably. "I say," Marco insisted, "that between the time Fuchs left the Strauss mansion and the time the car was wrecked on the highway, Fuchs pulled a switch, substituted another corpse to cover his trail."

"Why?" Brainard's question hung threateningly.

"Because Fuchs is General Reinhard Fuchs-Ohm, a logical assumption since he would have been in a position to know about donations to the Nazi war cause made by a handful of supposedly loyal American citizens."

"Bosh!" Brainard exclaimed. "Someone else was rifling the magic shop, got frightened when you showed and—"

"—and conveniently knew where to locate a can of cleaning fluid for starting a fire?"

"You expect me to provide an answer for every

detail?" Brainard challenged. "Denis Blaine killed the wrong man. I see it that way, and I imagine the court will have the same feeling."

"Soames admits he was working for Fuchs!" Marco protested.

"What if he does? That still establishes no connection between a magician and a Nazi general who disappeared ten years ago!"

"You refuse to believe Fuchs might have been the general?"

"I do. Damn it, Smith, if I dared bring up such a screwy notion, the commissioner would tack my hide to the wall and ticket me for the policemen's home. Absolutely the only evidence we have to support the connection is the word of Denis Blaine, an accused murderer."

"It happens that I believe his story," Marco said.

"He's your client."

"Point two," Marco insisted. "You refuse to believe Fuchs could still be alive?"

Brainard hesitated. "That could be possible. But where's the evidence?"

"Was anything found in the magic shop after the fire?"

"Nothing incriminating."

"Then the only evidence is that letter from Fuchs, posted after his death."

"*Signed* with the name of Fuchs," Brainard corrected.

"Would you make a search?" Marco asked. "If I

brought you the letter—if I could pry it away from Soames and place it in your hands—would you make a search for Fuchs to be certain he's not still alive?"

Brainard crumpled his hat on his head and thrust his jaw forward. He glared at the private detective. "All right, blast you. Produce the letter and I'll have a check made to locate Fuchs, though I know my men will be hunting for a big fat zero, a man made out of air. Richard Fuchs died in an auto crash." Halfway out of sight behind the screen, Brainard entered again and jabbed a finger in Marco's direction. "If I make the search, it will be your last bit of help. Remember that, Smith."

"The letter will be in your hands tonight."

Brainard shut the door with a slam. Marco swung his legs off the edge of the bed and thumbed the call button for the nurse. His legs smarted and itched beneath the dressings, and he still felt weary, but he wanted out.

"Please, Mr. Smith, please!" dithered the nurse on finding Marco standing barefooted beside the bed. Then her words died away, for she saw resolve on his face.

"Call the doctor," Marco said. "Pronto."


Harry Soames peered maudlinly into a schooner of beer. A juke, spraying an electric rainbow on the ceiling of the Atlas Bar and Grill, honked out a stomping saxophone tune. Soames shook his head and met the eyes of Marco Polo Smith, ashamed.

"I can't give you the letter, Mr. Smith. It's gone."

"What?" Marco cried.

"Last night after I left you, I dropped in at an all-night movie, trying to calm down. And when I arrived back at my room, oh, past midnight, I found all my clothes strewn on the floor, every dresser drawer emptied. Nothing had been taken except that letter. . . . Why did you want it?"

From the juke came a rising crescendo of jeering saxophone music. At the forward end of the bar, a drunken blonde laughed in a high, shrill voice.

"I wanted that letter to save a man's life," Marco said.


Marco stared at the telephone on his office desk. The phone was ringing for the sixth time. In shirt sleeves, sleepless all night, his legs a mass of irritation beneath bandages, Marco jerked the phone from its cradle and snarled, "Hello?"

"This is Brainard. What happened to your letter, my friend?"

Marco related the story.

"Then my hands are tied, Smith. If I were called on the carpet by the commissioner, what could I give him except hearsay evidence?"

"Soames worked for Fuchs! Isn't that—"

"Do you want me to arrest Soames and grill him?"

"I promised Soames the police wouldn't get him if he talked. I keep promises."

"Suit yourself. Keep out of my hair, though."

Marco crashed the phone on the cradle.

Two hours later, he faced Denis Blaine in the chill atmosphere of his cell in City Prison. Diana Meadows had arrived ten minutes before the detective, and now she listened to his story, a fur wrap drawn about her shoulders and a mounting shadow of dread clouding her eyes. Marco paced, emphasizing his points with stabs of a cigarette. Denis smiled politely but vacantly. Marco finished in a burst at the arrested man and his sweetheart:

"From your expressions, it's clear you think I've failed."

"Mr. Smith, we realize you tried . . ." Diana began.

"The leads are strong!" Marco thundered. "A ruthless mind is working against us. Stealing the letter. Blocking the search by the police. Perhaps I owe it to you to turn in Harry Soames. Yet what would he admit? That he had worked for Fuchs; that he had received a letter. So the police search. What would they find? Exactly nothing. The whole play smacks of a covered trail, a new disguise. Which

# THE DEVIL HAS FOUR FACES

the police will not trouble to hunt out. But I can try."

"How?" Denis asked bleakly.

"By finding the next victim! If the blackmailer is operating in this city, it's because there are other Germans, the traitorous few who donated money to Hitler's cause. Like Andrew, they'll be ready targets."

"Andrew . . ." Diana mused. "It seems incomprehensible that he—"

"He admitted it," Marco interrupted. "I have no interest in exposing his secret. What I must do now is find another person like Andrew, a person who is being bled. Then, maybe, we'll turn up General Reinhard Fuchs-Ohm."

Leaving City Prison, Marco realized that Denis Blaine and Diana Meadows didn't believe he could succeed. But he was more determined than ever to find the man who had tried to murder him in cold blood the night before.

# CHAPTER VI

Karl Strauss engaged a noted trial lawyer to provide Denis Blaine's defense, and Marco met with him over dinner to discuss the matter. The lawyer listened attentively to all the facts in Marco's possession, then pointed out that he could base no defense on merely a personal memory of a face from ten years in the past. The lawyer hoped to plan his defense around a study of the magician's face, which would be compared with a picture, if available, of the Nazi Fuchs-Ohm, to establish that Denis had indeed shot because of a mistake but with a very real motive. The lawyer related unhappily that he had been unable to unearth a picture of the general, even with the aid of the government in Washington. One confiscated German newsreel purportedly showed the general at a High-Command dinner in Berlin, but Hitler and Goering hogged the Nazi camera lens so theatrically that what was supposed to be the general's face showed up in the back of the stopped frame as a tiny, indistinct blur.

## THE DEVIL HAS FOUR FACES 91

If only, the lawyer exclaimed, the letter from Fuchs, dated after the shooting, had not been stolen!

Smith smiled thinly.

A young woman halted at a stairway entrance along one of the less savory thoroughfares of the city.

She peered uncertainly at a tiny scrap of paper, then raised her coarsely painted face to scrutinize a row of rusty tin plaques nailed up just inside the frame of the stairwell. At the bottom of the collection gleamed a sign which had not suffered the ravages of time. The new lettering informed her that Fritz Rohlwing, Photographer, could be found upstairs.

As she mounted the sour stairway, the woman's teeth began to chatter. She must hurry, she told herself. A few more hours and she would become a screaming maniac.

Her flimsy high-heeled pumps clattered on the squeaky floor of the upstairs hall. She couldn't have been more than thirty years old, but excessive make-up, the sick shadows of dissipation circling her eyes, and the gaudy sweater, skirt and coat she wore marred and cheapened her appearance. Tiny tremors began to tic in the flesh of her right cheek as she placed a trembling hand on the doorknob of the photographer's dark cubicle.

Entering, she paused in the tawdry reception room. Photographic prints of various cheery-faced subjects adorned the walls in a succession of peeling gilt-painted wooden frames. Each photo bore cracks on its dusty surface, as though it had been taken years before.

A man appeared from a rear room. Through the door behind him could be glimpsed an ancient camera, a dusty velvet-padded bench, the spindly shapes of a few spotlights on black iron poles.

But the young woman's attention was riveted on the newcomer, who smiled at her knowingly. He wore a soiled brown smock, and his hands were busy with a square of black cloth, diligently polishing a lens while he surveyed her.

"Mr. Rohlwing?"

The photographer nodded. Though he had a thin face, his cheeks appeared strangely puffed. His blue eyes loomed monstrously from behind thick lenses. Gray hair peeped out from beneath an obvious brown toupee and the man's cheeks seemed chalky, as though dusted with too much talcum. The wig, powder, and glasses transformed him into a figure not comic but grotesque and malignant—a wizened old lecher covering his age with cosmetics.

"Yah, I am Rohlwing. Your name is Nell Bluffton?"

The young woman nodded, nervously wiped a hand across her mouth. "Let's not waste time. I need the fix."

"Such a young creature," Rohlwing whispered, as if he enjoyed prodding her misery. "I have explained to our mutual acquaintance, the bartender, that I would expect—in return for a supply of drugs—performance of a task which is classed as criminal. Are you willing?"

A cynical smile played on the smeared lips. "There's hardly a thing I wouldn't do when I need fixing. Hardly a thing I haven't done, either," she amended.

Rohlwing chuckled. "Excellent. How do you require it?"

Nell Bluffton sucked in her breath, feeling the craving tighten its hold. "Main line."

"That can be arranged." The photographer lifted a thin gauze curtain at the entrance to the rear room. "Shall we step this way? My little assignment involves blackmail, my dear. Really quite tame. You shall contact a very wealthy and influential woman named Cheyney, here in the city." The photographer chuckled again, in private amusement. "The lady had a German husband, you see."

"No, I don't," Nell said. "All I know is that I need the stuff. Tell me what I must do. The sooner I start, the sooner I get relief."

Rohlwing headed in the direction of a battered roll-top desk. Nell Bluffton's eyes brightened, her breath grew sharper, her palms began to sweat. Sensing her eagerness, the man paused. His magnified eyes glittered in the poor light.

"Before I commit myself, I should point out that betrayal of my plan at any point would result in instantaneous suspension of your supply. You are no doubt aware it would be difficult to find another source. But should that punishment not be sufficiently severe, I would not hesitate to kill you. In any one of a number of most unpleasant ways."

Half-hypnotized, Nell Bluffton regarded the man fearfully. She was dimly frightened at the notion that she was committing herself to a bargain with a wholly vicious master. Still, the terrible sensations attacking her nerves grew worse each second. Her throat dried like parchment. Her temples burned.

"Please," she choked. "I understand. I agree."

The odd wigged head bobbed in a nod. Rohlwing took a key from his pocket and lifted the desk top with a clatter.

"Step this way, please. I am prepared for your visit."

On the following Sunday afternoon, Marco Smith took a taxi out along the six-lane through highway to the city's municipal stadium, to attend a football game.

Clear golden sunlight poured from a bright blue sky where veils of white cloud scooted in front of a crisp wind. A heavy crowd jammed the city park, which also served as home base for the city's major-league baseball team. Marco fell in with the lighthearted air of the spectators. He felt quite natty in his plaid topcoat and narrow-brimmed hat as he climbed the ramp to his seat. Around his neck dangled a leather carrying case which contained a pair of expensive Swiss binoculars. He settled into his seat and ordered a frankfurter from a shouting vendor.

While he munched on the wiener and bun, he unlimbered his glasses. But instead of scanning the white-lined green turf where the two teams warmed up, he focused the binoculars on a front-row box a dozen aisles below his own seat. The box was empty. Marco had been informed that the owner of the Stags never missed a home game. Perhaps she'd arrive late. He swung his glasses out onto the field as the teams cleared in preparation for the start of the game.

The Stags, white helmets and red jerseys sparkling in the sun, elected to receive. Marco settled down to enjoy the game amid the waving pennants and smells of smoke and hot coffee. In the first eight minutes of the first period, the Grizzlies scored twice against the Stags, for a total of 13 to 0. Marco shifted his binoculars, then caught his breath. Vy Cheyney—she had dropped the use of the name of her dead husband, Oscar Heinz, although she still held fast to ownership of his company, Heinz Beer—had arrived in her box. She sat alone, elbows on the rail, watching the game with frowning concentration.

Marco saw through the twin lenses a very handsome young woman, her bright auburn hair caught up in a silk scarf, a fur stole draped over the shoulders of a woolen dress which fitted her fine figure very well. She stood up to shout in protest when the Stag quarterback was dropped for a bad loss while attempting to pass, and Marco sensed over the intervening distance the power of her personality. In business circles she was reputed to be tough as iron. Oscar Heinz had married a young bride from a small dairy town, never dreaming he had found a woman who would—in a few brief years—understand his business better than he did. At least, so the stories ran.

Marco waited, curiously pleased to discover the woman so attractive. His gaze kept returning to her as the minutes ticked away. Even at a distance, he thought he saw a rare combination of beauty and brains. Her eyes flashed triumphantly when the Stags broke through for a touchdown and an extra point, and the gun went off signifying the end of play.

The crowd surged up, roaring. The scoreboard clock began to tick off the half period and Marco moved into the aisle. The Stags trotted off the field, six points behind. Vy Cheyney watched them with lightning in her cool green eyes as Marco slipped into the box and sat down beside her.

She swung around. When she realized a stranger had come unannounced into her box, her delicately

# THE DEVIL HAS FOUR FACES

arched eyebrows rose and one gloved hand clamped on the guardrail. Marco crossed his legs as though he belonged there.

Vy Cheyney said, "I believe you've walked into the wrong box."

Marco smiled. He shook his head, liking her voice in spite of its chilliness.

"No, I wanted to speak with you, Mrs. . . . Heinz?" he finished tentatively.

"Since my husband's death, I'm called Cheyney." She searched the stands for an usher, but the aisles were thronged with noisy spectators hurrying to the refreshment stands. She spun around again.

"I wanted to talk to you."

Disdain showed in the tilt of her nose. "I can't imagine why."

"Look, lady. I've been watching you through these glasses. You own the Stags, or at least your husband's brewery, Heinz Beer, owns them. It's natural for you to be sore when they have a sloppy defense and an even worse ground attack, but don't transfer the short temper to me. What I have to say is important."

Vy Cheyney cooled down a fraction. She took a cigarette from her handbag and pointedly refused Marco's offer of a light, using an expensive platinum lighter, instead. "Who are you?"

"Marco Polo Smith."

"Smith? The private detective? I've read about you in the papers." Her words conveyed boredom.

"I need no detective, Mr. Smith. And I'm growing a bit annoyed with your crude manner." She spotted a pair of ushers through a break in the crowd, raised her hand and signaled. The ushers moved rapidly toward the box. Vy Cheyney leaned back, smiling. "You were saying?"

Marco's tone became urgent. "Seriously, Miss Cheyney, it's very important . . ."

The ushers arrived. Evidently they had had previous experience with intruders in the boxes. Marco found himself being ejected forcibly while spectators turned curious eyes in his direction. He went along peacefully. The ushers shoved him into his seat.

"The lady don't like mashers hanging around, bud. Take a tip. Next time we really get rough."

When the game commenced its final half, Marco returned to a study of Vy Cheyney via binoculars. In their brief, hot-tempered interview, he had been fascinated by her physical charm. Now another factor haunted him elusively. While the crowd roared and chanted, he forgot the game and kept his glasses trained in her direction, until at last the will-o'-the-wisp quality registered.

Strain. That was it, sheer, nerve-wrenching strain.

It showed in the purplish shadows beneath her eyes, in the clenched tightness of her teeth, in the forward-leaning position of her taut body. Could she

## THE DEVIL HAS FOUR FACES

be so concerned about a football game? Hardly. After all, the Stags had chalked up a good record this season, and they had captured the conference championship the previous year. What other cares weighed her down, then? Not the affairs of Heinz Beer, another national giant, second of the three huge beer companies which made their headquarters in the city. All the financial columns testified to the success of the firm. Then what oppressed her?

Again through the binoculars he caught the tired tension of her face, and peculiarly, he felt stirrings of an interest which had no connection whatever with his prime purpose of the afternoon.

The Stags staged a third-quarter rally and as the clock showed four minutes left to play, Vy Cheyney's team led by a score of 20 to 13. Marco left his seat and hurried down through the stands to ground level. Locating an usher with a hungry face, Marco slipped him a five and asked where Miss Cheyney usually parked her automobile. With a leer, the usher directed him to one of the lots adjoining the stadium. The attendant on duty in this parking area, for another five, grudgingly pointed out a red Porsche Spyder as the property of Miss Vy Cheyney. Marco stood behind a neighboring limousine, lit a cigarette and waited for the crowd to come pouring out of the stands.

In the maze of honking horns, flaring tempers, and exhaust fumes, Vy Cheyney did not spot Marco until he vaulted into the seat beside her an instant before she started to steer the small car out of the lot.

"I am crudely persistent," he grinned.

Anger coated her cheeks with scarlet. She glanced about for help.

"If you pull that usher bit again," Marco warned, "I'll be forced to stage a brawl, sure to result in unwelcome publicity. Also, I had to snatch a cab out here. So while you give me a free ride back to the city, we can talk business."

"Where shall I drop you?" It was pure ice.

"Your place will be fine."

The young woman hesitated. Then a mysterious glint flitted in her green eyes. She started the car rolling forward. The traffic began to thin somewhat. Marco frowned. "What's the joke?"

He understood the joke all too clearly a moment later. She swung the Spyder onto the through highway. Her high-heeled foot rammed down on the gas pedal. The sports car leaped forward with an alarming burst of power and the tachometer shot up close to eighty. She wove the little auto in and out through three lanes of traffic funneling toward the city. The Spyder shot through an opening between two massive sedans. Marco gasped.

She laughed mockingly. The scarf around her hair whipped in the wind. Above the keening noise, she cried, "Enjoying the ride, Mr. Smith? We have seven more miles before we reach my apartment."

# THE DEVIL HAS FOUR FACES

Marco met her challenging gaze with a grin of his own. Clearly she meant to scare him. Her hands manipulated the wheel deftly, spinning it split seconds before each seemingly impending crash. Drivers craned their heads in astonishment. The Spyder whizzed drunkenly from lane to lane, holding eighty.

Marco lifted his foot, placed it on top of hers, and exerted pressure.

Vy Cheyney attempted to extricate her foot. The tachometer zoomed to ninety and did not stop. Marco kept his foot firmly in place, laughing. Vy had no time for anger. She was completely occupied with managing the runaway automobile.

"Wonderful ride!" Marco shouted.

The needle climbed higher still.


At that same time, in the gloom of Vy Cheyney's nine-room apartment in the Edinburgh Arms, Mr. Casper Tolenado crossed his legs, creased his trouser seam sharply and lighted a menthol cigarette.

Mr. Tolenado sat quietly waiting, a thin, unpleasantly pale man with sunken cheeks. A flower gleamed in his buttonhole. In one hand he juggled the skeleton key with which he had entered the apartment. In his lap, touched by a ray of fading sunlight which fell through a slit between draperies, a long, wicked-looking automatic gleamed dull blue. Mr. Tolenado passed a scented hand across his dark hair. Then he hefted the automatic lovingly, a smile on his wet pink lips.

Strolling along the richly carpeted hallway in the swank Edinburgh Arms, Marco was completely ignored by Vy Cheyney. As she inserted a key in her door, Marco propped himself against the wall and rattled:

"The brewery business has always struck me as pretty colorful. Rich in culture, if you know what I mean. Why, I wonder if your public-relations staff at Heinz knows the etymology of the term bock beer? Heinz turns out a fair bock every March; they should be informed. Well, bock originated in the town of Einbeck, Germany, about the year twelve hundred." Vy proceeded into the apartment, attempting to slam the door. Marco followed her in. "Beer named for the town, but language becomes corrupted. Einbeck became ein bock, a goat. Everyone uses the goat logo on the label these days. I like bock. One third wheat malt, two thirds barley malt, very dark, deliciously sweet. I—"

Vy Cheyney blocked his passage through the foyer. She faced Marco. "Must I resort to telephoning the police? I'm sick of your following me like some sort of mooning hound, and I demand that you stop this idiotic, revolting—"

Marco hissed, "Hold it!"

Over her shoulder, in the vaguely outlined living

# THE DEVIL HAS FOUR FACES

room, a form rose, advanced, and a white blur became an unpleasant effeminate face. Marco stepped aside. Vy breathed a little gasp, and her face faded to chalky paleness. The visitor gave an unpleasant grimace of embarrassment as he clumsily juggled an automatic out of sight beneath his coat. The scent of toilet water filled the air.

"Excuse me, Miss Cheyney," the visitor said. "Never dreaming you'd have a guest, I took the liberty of unlocking your door. It's most urgent that we talk."

Vy teetered on the edge of fury. "Go back to Gregory, Mr. Tolenado, and tell him we have already talked quite enough. You know my attitude."

Tolenado licked his lips. "This becomes very unpleasant for me."

"Is that why you brought your gun?" Vy demanded. Marco's nerves tightened a notch.

"Yes! Either you agree to the demands, or you'll find yourself in genuine trouble." The man's white hand stirred suggestively toward the breast pocket of his suit. "If you could arrange for your gentleman friend to leave us alone, we could come to terms."

Marco moved forward. "Hang it up," he said softly. His thumb jerked in the direction of the doorway.

Tolenado smiled mincingly. "Kindly don't interfere where you don't belong."

"Out, sweetheart. Fast. Your perfume smells."

Like a streak, Tolenado's hand dived beneath his coat. Marco speared his arm with both hands, levered, and used Tolenado's wrist to crack the whip. The man crashed against the closed hall door. Seething, Tolenado slipped into a crouch and inched forward. Once more, he went for his gun. Marco threw a right that slammed Tolenado's head into the door panel. Tolenado swayed and shook his head. Marco knotted his fist in the man's coat and dragged him down the hall toward the elevator. When the car arrived Marco prodded Tolenado forward with the man's own automatic. Tolenado rested against the car wall, rubbing his bruised jaw.

"You can be fixed," he sneered. "You will be."

"Cheap words," said Marco. The elevator door clanged shut.

Marco returned to the apartment with Tolenado's automatic in his pocket. In the living room Vy had drawn back the draperies. Pale golden sunlight spilled between skyscrapers and dappled the carpet. Marco watched as Vy strode toward a wall bar and poured herself a vigorous portion of bourbon. She added soda, and Marco helped himself to the same. Sinking onto a divan, Vy Cheyney exhibited her first sign of humanity. She smiled in an apologetic way.

"Sorry, Mr. Smith. You shouldn't have become involved. Tolenado is a very dirty man."

# THE DEVIL HAS FOUR FACES

Marco nodded. "He's a cheap hoodlum. Why are you mixed up with him?"

Irony twisted her lips and distorted the clearness of her green eyes. "Because of an eight-year-old child," she said cryptically. "But, please, Tolenado is a problem I must work out for myself."

"Why not call the police?"

Vy hesitated, gripping her drink. "I can't."

"Shall we talk about my business, then?"

She agreed with a nod of her head.

"The questions I want to ask," Marco said, "may strike a nerve or two. But a man's life may be staked on the answers you give me. Are you familiar with the Blaine case—the shooting of the magician Fuchs?"

"Quite familiar. I've followed it in the papers. I know Diana Meadows. I know her uncle, Karl Strauss, even better." She feigned a smile. "The local brewing industry sticks together you see. What possible connection could I have with the case?"

"Your husband, Miss Cheyney, was a very wealthy German-American citizen of this city. I must ask whether any circumstances have ever caused you to believe that during the second World War he might have donated money secretly to the Nazi cause." Sudden wariness glinted in the green eyes. Afraid she would panic to silence, Marco rushed on: "The Blaine case is hinged on a blackmailer of important persons who gave secret funds to the Nazis."

"Are you working for Blaine?"

"In his behalf. Diana Meadows hired me."

Vy hesitated. "I—I didn't marry Oscar Heinz until nineteen forty-six. He died four years later. How could I have known about any donations?"

Marco leaned forward. "The blackmailer is operating today. I think he might have presented you with photostats . . ." Here, Marco skated on thin ice, but the truth he saw in her eyes prodded him forward. "Pages from a book written in German, showing the amount of donations, the dates, through what channels the donations were made."

A match flared. Vy's hand shook slightly as she lit her cigarette. "You're wrong. You spoke of the blackmailer as a man. It's a woman."

"Who?"

"Nell Bluffton is her name. She approached me four days ago, at my office. She did have photostats." Vy gazed at Marco directly. "Mr. Smith, if what I tell you leaks out, it will spell disaster for Heinz Beer."

"That's the beautiful secret of the whole dirty plot," Marco agreed. "What happened when this Bluffton woman called? Did you pay her?"

"How much of this," Vy countered quickly, "do you intend to repeat?"

"Nothing, if it leads me to the person I want."

"Very well. In—in spite of all my nasty words at the stadium, I owe you a favor for your help with Tolenado. The Bluffton woman showed me three

# THE DEVIL HAS FOUR FACES

photostats such as you described. My husband apparently made three deposits, totaling forty-two thousand dollars, all through the Swiss Credit Bank Universal located in Basel." Another wan smile. "Poor Oscar. He was a gentle little man. Like a child. He sold millions of dollars' worth of beer each year, and yet I had to tell him what sort of foods he should eat, and remind him what size shoes he wore. And eventually I learned enough to coach him on what stocks to buy. He could easily have made such a donation. I think he'd have regretted his action by now, but that wouldn't alter the grim appearance of the record. During the war, though, he often talked in a sentimental way about the *vaterland*."

Marco sat down beside Vy. Forcing his mind to concentrate, he said, "Did the Bluffton woman ask for money?"

"Yes. She demanded a semi-monthly installment of one thousand dollars. The first payment comes due in two days. The woman is supposed to visit the Heinz plant and slip into a group taking the nine-thirty public tour. I'm to meet her somewhere along the route, and pass her the cash." Vy shook her head. "She's sure, very sure. Or her employer is, at least. She told me she had instructions to call at the plant every other week, to make the payments easy for me."

"Will you pay?"

"My personal answer was no. The board of directors said yes, however. I only control thirty-six per cent of the voting stock."

Marco reached out and seized her hand. She did not draw away. "Let me corner this Bluffton woman. I'll be very careful, but I have to get back to the person for whom she's working. This may be a way . . ." Marco found himself suddenly pouring out the whole story of the Blaine case, and at the end, her face mirrored belief. "Now you can see why it's so vital to Denis Blaine," he concluded.

After a moment, Vy Cheyney said softly, "I'll help you."

As night deepened across the city, Vy Cheyney drew a bath and lay back in the hot scented water, eyes closed, recalling the detective's face.

What strange transmutation had altered their relationship so quickly from antagonism to a . . . a peculiar warmth which she thought had escaped her forever? He made a tough, giddy figure, this Smith, in his plaid overcoat, wisecracking, digging up the etymology of bock beer, smacking down the warped Tolenado in the gloom of the foyer. The problem of Gregory, of Virginia, still loomed like a threatening cloud. Yet, as the scented steam rose up to envelop her, she hummed a tune. All at once, she felt that she still might be young after all.

# CHAPTER VII

Mr. Caspar Tolenado leaned loosely upon a white-painted rail fence, picked his teeth and suppressed his irritation as a snarling bullet-bodied green racer cut around the brick track on singing rubber.

The track had been especially built at the fringe of the country estate belonging to Gregory Thiess, owner of the Thiess Brewery, third of the city's great brewing triumvirate and producer of Heidelberg Lager. The Thiess property, with all its sprawling acreage, its vast colonial house, its swimming pool, tennis courts, stable and special racing garage and auto track, was situated some six miles from the edge of the city. This fact constantly annoyed Tolenado, who was forced to drive the distance to report in person to the man paying his salary. The moment Tolenado thought in specific terms of the amount of that salary, however, he changed his tune and lost his reservations. Thiess had sought him out through devious underworld channels, and the wages he received—even if violence became necessary, as Thiess intimated—were ample.

Nevertheless, Mr. Caspar Tolenado rankled at being kept waiting while the millionaire brewery owner indulged his enthusiasm for privately built racers. Mincing his lips in disapproval, Tolenado watched the green automobile complete another circuit at blinding speed. Atop a small frame observation stand built beside the track, a flunky signaled with a crisscross motion of a colored flag. The racer wheeled past the tower once more as the checkered flag came down, then took a final turn to slow the speed. When the car came around again and stopped before the tower, additional flunkies rushed out to congratulate the white-helmeted man climbing from the car's cockpit.

Caspar Tolenado flung his toothpick aside and strolled toward the wooden building. He refrained from approaching Thiess while the latter was still surrounded by his servants. At last, however, Thiess came through the gate in the fence, mopping his neck with a heavy towel. A Negro climbed into the racer and drove it toward the garages built on the side of an adjoining hill.

Tolenado shivered, for a sharp breeze cut the autumn sunlight. Gregory Thiess, on the other hand, seemed indifferent to the chill, dressed in white jodhpurs and jersey, white crash helmet hanging from one meaty hand. He slung his towel over his shoulder and greeted Tolenado with his own peculiar brand of a smile—a smirk.

"News?" Thiess muttered through his thick, purplish lips.

Tolenado responded with a nod. "That's the reason I drove all the way out here. I thought your men signaled you on the track. What I have to say is urgent."

With one great paw, Thiess slapped the hoodlum on the back. Tolenado uttered a cry of pained surprise. Thiess guffawed. "Then drive me up to the house. We can discuss it there."

Tolenado wrenched open the door of his inexpensive sedan and Thiess climbed in. He was a stout man with a large head and bushy hair running to gray. The rather stupid, jowlish cast of his face was offset by a shrewd, unpleasant brilliance in his small blue eyes. While Tolenado thumbed the starter button, Thiess displayed one of the glowering frowns which made him absolute master of the men who labored throughout the Heidelberg Lager organization.

Thiess spoke heavily: "Tolenado, I pay you a hundred dollars a day. Resentment is not one of your fringe benefits."

"Okay! If you want to get nasty, I'll be glad to refrain from taking any more lumps from Marco Smith."

Wrinkles of concentration lined Thiess' brow. "Smith? Marco . . . Smith?"

Tolenado gnashed the gears, shifting up the dirt road which wound around a hillside back toward the Thiess mansion. "A private detective. A smart private detective with a fast set of knuckles. When I called on Miss Cheyney yesterday," Tolenado went on, "I found her entertaining a stranger—Smith. He threw me out, marked up my face with these bruises. When I collected my wits I remembered I had seen this fellow's picture before. Marco Polo Smith. Trouble."

Thiess swung around in the seat. A string of profanity fell from his lips. He smacked an angry fist against the dashboard. "What a hell of a day!" he snarled. "I bettered my record with the Green Piston Special by more than four seconds, and then you tell me that Vy has hooked up with a private detective!"

Tolenado said nothing.

Thiess continued to fume. Finally he roared, "I wish you'd take a bath before you come out here. That—perfume you use makes me sick. Repulsive! That a man should soak himself in—"

"Let's not get personal, please," Tolenado hissed. "I gave you credit for intelligence, Mr. Thiess. Why switch your petulance to me? Cheyney hired the dick; I didn't."

"You think Vy is paying him to protect her?"

Tolenado gave a shrug. "Why else would he hang around? . . . Besides, what other course does she have? I've already made two—ah—proposals. I've

# THE DEVIL HAS FOUR FACES

even promised that she might come to physical harm if she failed to comply with your wishes. Certainly she can't contact the police, for the same reason that you can't institute court action. If the child were—"

"Shut up," Thiess exploded. "Shut your silly mouth and let me think."

Tolenado obeyed. They arrived at the massive white Thiess mansion, which crowned the summit of a high green hill. In the distance, banks of wintry gray clouds formed. Thiess, the eternal aging athlete, ran puffily up the broad steps. Tolenado followed. In the library, where a private stock market ticker clicked away the rise and fall of big business, Thiess drew on a thick blue sweater provided by his butler, and settled down to face his hired hoodlum.

"More delay!" he raged, slapping the desk.

"Smith is certainly an obstacle," Tolenado agreed.

"Why can't she die?" Thiess fumed, his small eyes remote. "Why can't she be struck by a car? How does that old ballad go? '. . . and a rope from hell to hang her.' I wish a rope would drop out of heaven and throttle her beautiful neck!"

"I serve in place of heaven," Tolenado said. A warped smile touched his effeminate face.

"We should have done it in the first place. Now this detective is tagging along."

"Let me handle it."

"How?"

"By removing the detective. Let the accident happen to Smith, and Vy Cheyney may realize the seriousness of her position. If Smith died suddenly, it might shock her into turning the child over to you. Either that, or we could kidnap the child from the orphanage, if you like."

"I told you before, no kidnapping! I must have a signed paper giving me custody. I can keep the paper in my safe. If word of that child leaks out, Tolenado, I'd be ruined."

Tolenado did not care. His mind was suddenly obsessed with the notion of repaying Marco Smith for attacking him yesterday. "Then my orders are to eliminate the detective?"

Thiess took the leap. "Yes, go ahead. But remember," he cautioned, "if you foul things up, you'll get no cover from me. Keep your nose clean on this, but more important, keep me clean. Clear?"

Tolenado rose. "Very clear. You'll have a report." He left the room hastily, a sadistic smile in his eyes.

Gregory Thiess stared after him. The stock ticker chattered monotonously. Out of habit, Thiess tore off the tape, but flung it in a wastebasket without a second glance.

He wandered to the French windows and stared out across the vista of chilly countryside and bare, stark trees outlined against the sky. He did not relish association with Tolenado. Yet what choice

## THE DEVIL HAS FOUR FACES

remained? Thiess told himself that his back was against the wall. The house of sand—the house of tricky financial dealings, of dummy accounts, of fake holding firms built over the years—had begun to crumble. In his greed to amass money, Thiess had formed an engine of destruction. While he took action on a number of fronts, the child, Virginia Brown, represented his primary avenue of salvation. Thiess returned to his desk and drew an unmounted photo from the bottom drawer.

He scowled at the portrait of the charming eight-year-old girl and tried to reconstruct the circumstances which had made it possible for him to enter into a love affair with a hellcat like Vy Cheyney. For a time, their secret meetings had brought him happiness. Then, with the announcement of the coming child, they had quarreled, split up, grown to hate each other. Thiess had gladly surrendered secret custody of the child to Vy at birth. Vy had flown to Canada, away from her husband, on a doctor's faked recommendation that she needed special sanatorium care. The child had been placed in an orphanage at the age of one month, well cared for by Vy, forgotten by Thiess, until— Damn! he thought again.

How many secrets could a man carry in his heart without going insane? The child, the financial tangle, the way he had forced a former chairman of the board to suicide, the donations to the Nazis—

so many skeletons, each one capable of damning him completely if it ever came to light. At the moment, though, the matter of Virginia Brown was the most pressing.

The telephone startled him. He answered, and found his lawyer, Arthur Southart, on the wire.

"Gregory? Has Vy given over custody?"

"No, not yet, but—"

"Damn it, man," Southart said, "we have only a few more days! When the right moment has passed, we don't have another chance to use the girl. We have to transfer holdings, manipulate the whole Thiess Brewery tax structure, set up new subsidiaries. That takes time, time! You fail to realize just how vital your custody of this child—"

"I know exactly how vital it is!" Thiess screamed into the phone. "Now quit dogging me, Southart. I'm doing the best I can!"

He slammed the telephone down. At that moment, the butler knocked discreetly.

Thiess straightened his face as the butler rolled Gretta Thiess into the room. Her shrunken, birdlike body and vacant smile revolted him as she sat huddled in her wheelchair. In the lap of her rusty black silk dress her blue-veined hands toyed with one of the crocheted mottoes on which she spent all her waking hours. The motto read, *God Is Love*.

At thirty-nine years of age, she was totally crippled. Thiess walked over and kissed his wife's withered hand.

"Gregory," she asked, smiling, "when are you going to take me to church?"

"This Sunday, darling. This Sunday, I promise faithfully."

While she chattered on, showing him the tiny rosebuds she had crocheted around the rim of the motto, his thoughts wheeled back to Tolenado and the plan to do away with the detective. Smiling with vacant obedience down into the vapid face of his wife, he thought, If you only knew that at this very moment I am becoming a murderer!

"This ain't a public telephone booth," snapped the white-jacketed owner of the Atlas Bar and Grill, handing over the instrument which had rung on the back bar a moment earlier.

He thrust a beefy thumb in the direction of the public telephone at the rear of the room. "Run your office from there, pal, after this."

An expression of disdain crossed the features of Harry Soames as he hoisted the receiver to his ear.

"Hello? Oh, Mr. Smith. What? Hang on a second—the juke is blowing up a storm in here." Soames cupped a palm over his free ear to blot out the thundering rhythm of one of the popular hits of the day. "Tomorrow morning? Help you follow a dame? Would I! Absolutely. W-what?

"Twenty bucks? Heaven, absolute heaven. I'm beginning to recover from the scare that rat Fuchs threw into me with his letter. Say . . . what's turned up on him? Oh, no can talk? Okay, shoot me the dope tomorrow morning. Nine-fifteen, at the main entrance. I'll be there. So long, Mr. Smith."

Summoning his first grin in several days, Harry Soames snapped his fingers. The bartender approached skeptically. "One bottle of Heinz Beer," Soames announced. "Tomorrow I am again legitimate."

"Impossible," muttered the bartender.

Nothing disturbed Harry Soames, however. Only when he returned to his frowsy room did he discover that his wandering hands had spirited away from the Atlas Bar and Grill an empty beer bottle, two napkins, and a tumbler. With a tiny sigh of regret, he deposited these items on a flimsy table, stretched out on the iron bed and closed his eyes.


A brisk northwest wind stiffened the American flag flying above the Heinz Brewery administration quadrangle at nine-thirty next morning. Marco Polo Smith and Harry Soames had just come through the gate in the wake of a group of college students from a nearby university. Manufacturing buildings spread out around them in every direction. Other guides channeled the group into a dimly lighted auditorium. Marco sank into one of the thickly cushioned seats. As Harry Soames sat down, a peculiar clanking and rattling issued from the folds of his overcoat.

"What's all that racket?" Marco asked.

Soames went into his pockets. Clear bewilderment shone on his face as he produced three spoons, a fork, the lid from a sugar bowl, four pennies, half a cigar butt, and a white lace cap. Soames dangled this final item before Marco, nearly blushing.

"The—the waitress where I got breakfast laid this on the counter when some grease from the grill spattered on it. But I don't remember picking it up."

"Does your coat always contain such an assortment of knicknacks?" Marco laughed.

Soames nodded unhappily. "My hands are screwy, that's all. Pick up everything in sight. Someday, when I roll up enough cash, the best psychiatrist in the U.S.A. is going to work me over and take this kleptomania out of my nut. You'd be amazed at the jams I land in, just because—"

Marco seized his companion's arm. "Hold it!"

Soames followed the detective's glance. Nell Bluffton had just slipped into a seat in the adjacent section.

The young woman's dyed hair and excessive makeup clashed with the tasteful decor of the auditorium and the generally refined nature of the crowd, a mixture of students, well-dressed visitors and nattily attired guides. Nell Bluffton flung furtive glances over the crowd and began to bite her nails while a suave gray-haired company executive mounted the rostrum and welcomed the thirty-odd visitors. After delivering a four-minute plug for the brewing industry in general and Heinz in particular, the executive summoned forward one of the male guides.

"May I present Mr. Sommers, who will conduct your tour. You are all cordially invited to lunch in our Hospitality House this noon when you complete the trip. I hope you'll find your visit with the Heinz Brewery family interesting and rewarding. Thank you, and good morning."

"Thanks a heap," Marco breathed dryly. The crowd rose and assembled around Sommers, the guide. Marco never swung his eyes from Nell Bluffton. Vy Cheyney had described her remarkably well. Marco and Soames had no difficulty in keeping track of her, since she tended to hang nervously at the rear of the group.

As the crowd climbed a flight of stairs into the brew house nearly an hour later, Sommers had not once stanched his flow of propaganda: "The huge copper kettles you glimpse just ahead, ladies and gentlemen, act as giant percolators. They process the fine grains you saw in the malt storage bins at the beginning of our tour. To the grains, at this stage . . ."

Up ahead, talking with a white-coated foreman, Marco spotted Vy Cheyney. Nell Bluffton saw her, too.

# THE DEVIL HAS FOUR FACES

". . . are added only first-quality hops. Here, as everywhere, Heinz prides itself on cleanliness. You'll notice the gleaming metal, and the floors. If lunch hadn't been planned for the Hospitality House, why, we might serve it off the floor." A mild titter ran through the group. Only Marco, Harry Soames, and Nell Bluffton did not smile.

As the group moved on, Vy broke away from the foreman. She smiled and geeeted the guide in a pleasant fashion. Her eyes caught Marco's for a moment. Neither made any sign of recognition. Marco noticed the large white envelope Vy carried in one hand.

"Walk faster," Marco whispered to Soames. "The woman is . . . Yes! She dropped her handbag. She's falling back a moment. Eyes straight ahead. Don't turn around."

For several seconds they continued with the group. Then Marco glanced at Nell Bluffton. Perspiration had popped out on her forehead. She clutched the white envelope in one hand and mopped her brow with the other.

At the end of the tour, Nell Bluffton broke away from the group at the entrance to the chalet-like Hospitality House. Marco watched her disappear into the plant guard's cubicle. "Parking lot," he shot at Harry Soames. "She's using the telephone, probably calling a cab."

The pursuit quickened. Through heavy traffic,

they followed the taxi which carried Nell Bluffton. Marco turned to his companion.

"The next step I can carry out alone, Harry. There might be gunplay."

"You hired me," Soames said. "This is my first break in a long while, Mr. Smith. I'll stick, if you don't have any objections."

Marco grinned. "Okay. Oh-oh. The cab has stopped."

Marco swung the wheel of his car. Ahead the taxi had deposited Nell Bluffton before a stairway which led into a run-down building. Marco climbed from the car. The neighborhood was squalid. Nell Bluffton disappeared up the stairs. Marco and Harry moved along the sidewalk.

At the bottom of the stairs Marco noticed a new name plate announcing the presence of Fritz Rohlwing, Photographer. The plate stood out conspicuously among its ancient fellows. They climbed the rickety stairs two at a time. From his shoulder holster Marco snaked his .38 and carried it cupped in the side pocket of his overcoat, ready.

Exactly fifteen seconds behind Marco Smith, Caspar Tolenado braked his automobile and leaped out. His effeminate face shone with cruel eagerness as he rushed along the sidewalk toward the stair entrance. He did not know where Smith and his companion were going, but Tolenado wanted to

# THE DEVIL HAS FOUR FACES

settle his score with the detective. He peered up into the gloom of the hallway. Beneath his coat was a massive .45.

As he climbed, the old heady urge to destroy seized his brain, dizzying him. His eyelids drooped low, malevolently.

# CHAPTER VIII

A distant, rhythmic tap of high heels arrested the attention of Fritz Rohlwing. He swung around in his squeaking swivel chair and craned to view the entrance of his shop. Momentarily Rohlwing threw a glance at the slender leather volume resting open on the scarred surface of the roll-top desk. He took one final glance at the pages, finely written in German, snapped off the light, and carried the closed book with him into the front of the shop.

A shadow fell across the threshold. The overhead bell tinkled. Nell Bluffton entered quickly.

Rohlwing's blue eyes slitted, alert and suspicious. The young woman showed every sign of being close to nervous collapse. Her lips quivered. Her eyes glistened with a watery film. Her hands trembled at the clasp of her cheap alligator bag.

The photographer dropped his book on top of a glass display case and his viselike hand whipped out, gripping her wrist. "Collect yourself!" he ordered.

Nell Bluffton wrenched back and forth, approaching hysteria. Vainly she tried to break the man's powerful hold. "Please, oh please," she burbled. "Please help me, Mr. Rohlwing. My nerves are going to pieces . . . If I don't get relief right away, I'll go out of my mind."

A cynical smile curved the man's mouth. "That I doubt. What happened at the Heinz factory? Did you bungle? If you carried on as you are now, I can imagine the sight you presented." Nell Bluffton continued her tormented sobbing. Rohlwing raised his free hand and blistered it across her cheek.

She staggered against the wall. Rohlwing advanced, a menacing frown on his brow.

"Did you collect the payment? What a lunatic I was to trust a tramp like you!"

Nell Bluffton seized his coat. "Here it is, Mr. Rohlwing! Here!" She tore open her handbag and produced the envelope given her by Vy Cheyney. Then she slumped to her knees on the floor. Strands of dyed hair drooped down over her face as her sobbing rose. "I only . . . only act this way because I've gone so long without . . . I need . . . Oh, please, Mr. Rohlwing, let me . . . back room . . ."

Paying no attention to her, Rohlwing was ripping open the envelope when a rapid-fire series of running footsteps clattered along the hallway outside.

Instantly he produced a squat pistol from within the dusty showcase. He stuffed the white envelope into a pocket of his tan smock. Two more shadows fell across the closed frosted door. Rohlwing concealed the pistol, jerked Nell Bluffton to her feet and planted her with a brutal shove in a dusty wicker chair in one corner. He took up a post directly behind a display cabinet as the little bell above the door tinkled.

The instant Rohlwing spotted his visitors, he threw one glance at Nell Bluffton and made up his mind that he would be forced to kill her.

For a fleeting instant Nell Bluffton noted the photographer's peculiar expression. Her wracked face broke in a pattern of horrific understanding and dumb protest. She whipped her eyes desperately to the pair of strangers. Rohlwing bowed from the hips and smiled ingratiatingly. He had recognized both Marco Polo Smith and the ferret-faced Soames. But he showed not a trace of recognition.

"Something I can do for you gentlemen?" Rohlwing inquired. He ignored the .38 which Marco held casually at his side.

Marco threw Rohlwing a tough glance. "Take off the wig and glasses, my friend. Let's see what's underneath."

Rohlwing blinked. "Again, *bitte?* I do not comprehend your request."

Marco turned and looked at Nell Bluffton. "Where is the envelope of cash you took from Miss Cheyney at the Heinz plant?"

# THE DEVIL HAS FOUR FACES

Before Nell could frame a reply, Rohlwing burst out: "May I know the meaning of this outrage? Miss Bluffton called at my studio for the purpose of having a portrait made. What right have you to charge into my quarters, shouting, bellowing, waving a pistol, badgering my customers?" Rohlwing gesticulated wildly.

"Quiet, Rohlwing, if that's your name. Let the lady speak," Marco said.

Nell Bluffton half-rose from her chair, quavering. She opened her mouth. Then Marco saw her eyes widen, her greasy red lips form the first syllables of a scream.

"Watch the gun, Mr. Smith!" Soames shouted.

A cracking explosion rocked the air. Rohlwing scuttled into the rear room of the shop as Nell Bluffton struck the floor, her scream forever stilled, her mouth a foaming welter of blood. Abruptly, a peculiar silence enveloped the shop.

Marco was concentrating on the ill-defined blackness of the rear quarters, yet he heard the gagging sound which marked the young woman's death. Then he vaulted toward the opening, Soames at his heels.

Through the doorway, he stumbled into three tall iron poles. One of the pole stands tipped, the heavy spotlight atop it plummeting down. Marco ducked and charged forward as the massive light crashed inches behind him. "Cripes!" Soames shouted, dodging out of line.

From out of the darkness spat an orange streak of flame. Marco went to the floor and Soames fell with him.

He waited, heard no sound of movement, and began carefully crawling forward.

A widening vertical strip of light flooded into the gloomy loft for a split second. Marco leaped to his feet. The figure of Fritz Rohlwing, carrying a thin book in one hand, leaped out in silhouette against the sky for a moment. Then Rohlwing closed the metal door from the opposite side. Marco shouted while running forward:

"Soames? You all right?"

"Keep after him," Soames yelled. "He never touched me."

Marco pushed through the door and emerged on a rickety fire escape.

The ladder had already begun the slow automatic swing up into place. Marco's eyes swept a rabbit warren of tenement yards spread out below. No sign of movement. Gingerly he started down the weighted stair. When he had descended halfway, two shots rang out. Marco flattened against the wall. Brick dust stung his cheeks. Before there was a chance to remain a target, he gripped the stair railing and vaulted to the alley below.

Trying to right himself vainly as he fell, Marco struck the pavement with one leg twisted beneath him. He attempted to rise, and his ankle gave way in a stab of pain. Once more, he made the effort,

# THE DEVIL HAS FOUR FACES

aware that with each wasted second his quarry was slipping farther away. He hobbled slowly in the direction of the board fence, on the other side of which stood the rubbish pile from whose cover Rohlwing had fired. Marco found an opening and emerged into the yard just as a woman's piercing shriek keened out from one of the tenements. He struggled up the broken stairway and through the tenement corridor to the next street. Brief questions to the woman cowering in the hallway served to tell him that Rohlwing had dodged through to the street outside, brandishing his pistol. When Marco reached the stoop of the dismal tenement, he confronted a curious crowd of urchins and loafers already gathering on the sidewalk. There was no sign of Rohlwing.

Marco trudged back through the tenement and painfully scaled the fire escape, secure in the knowledge that four different people on the street had dutifully reported Rohlwing vanishing in three different directions. Failure smarted in Marco's mind as he picked his way through the rubble of the camera studio. Soames was nowhere in sight. Marco called his name.

"Out here," came the ex-detective's response from the front of the shop. He sounded queerly stifled.

Chewing his lips against the pain, Marco rounded the corner of the doorframe into the picture-lined room.

Harry Soames faced one wall, hands raised. Inches away, Caspar Tolenado smiled unpleasantly, a .45 weighing one gloved hand.

"Step in, Mr. Smith," Tolenado purred. "I heard the firing a few moments ago."

"What the hell is this?" Smith blazed.

"Only that you have intruded where you do not belong," Tolenado whispered. The muzzle of the .45 swung around in a slow, precise arc. "I suggest you drop that .38. Drop it straight down onto the floor, Mr. Smith."

Marco knew that he was facing death as he looked into Tolenado's eyes.

Tolenado repeated his words: "The gun, Mr. Smith. Drop it."

Marco snapped his wrist up alongside his trouser leg and pressured the trigger of his .38.

A spot of blood widened on Tolenado's light topcoat. His legs wavered and his face screwed into a mask of bitter anger. With a monumental effort, he attempted to raise his .45, trying to set up a final shot. Harry Soames pivoted neatly on one heel and chopped the .45 away.

The killer rotated slowly on corkscrew legs. His eyes rolled up in his head, leaving his pupils blank and white for an instant. Then he pitched over, moaning. Marco kicked the .45 out of range with the toe of his shoe.

He and Soames exchanged weak smiles.

"Who . . ." Soames was forced to swallow and phrase his question again. "Who was that joker?"

Marco shook his head. "A man I had to rough up a few days ago. Why he suddenly decided I had to be killed I don't know. But I intend to ask him when he wakes up." Marco knelt, peeled off Tolenado's overcoat and opened his shirt. A quick examination told him that Tolenado was losing a great deal of blood. Marco motioned Soames toward the door.

"What a mess! Rohlwing gone, the Bluffton girl dead, Tolenado gunning for me . . ."

Soames' eyes rounded. "Tolenado? Is that clown on the floor Caspar Tolenado?" When Marco gave an affirmative nod, Soames whistled and exclaimed, "Poison!"

Marco telephoned Captain Brainard from a corner cigar store. "I want to talk with nobody but Brainard," he told the answering sergeant.

Twelve minutes later, the police arrived. Soames led them to the shop but made no comment until Marco and Captain Brainard shouldered in. Brainard scowled at the bloodstains. Soames, hardly able to contain himself any longer, swallowed and stared at the floor. Marco's double take registered with Brainard, who growled, "What the hell is so surprising?"

"Tolenado is gone!"

"What? You mean Caspar Tolenado, the hood?"

"That's right. He turned up here. Tried to kill

me. I shot him, left him lying here, badly injured. Now he's gone."

At three-thirty in the afternoon, in the gloom-ridden streets visible through the windows of Captain Brainard's dusty office, fat wet flakes of snow drifted down through an oppressive sky. Fluorescent fixtures in the office ceiling cast pitiless white light on Brainard's scarred, ash-spattered oak desk. An ornately framed likeness of the police commissioner, hanging on one of the cracked plaster walls, stared vapidly at the snow. The metal radiator hissed and clanked. Cigar smoke hung in the air. Brainard, in shirt sleeves, head bent over a blue-ruled tablet, finally threw his pencil aside.

Rising wearily, the police officer sighed and ripped off the top sheet of the pad. This he placed in a desk drawer which contained his report forms. As he rolled down the sleeves of his rumpled white shirt and commenced reknotting his tie, he said heavily, "Well, there are no holes in your story, I regret to say."

Soames had been released an hour earlier. Only Marco remained, perched on the window sill, smoking as he looked at the snowy streets below.

"The only course left is to release you," Brainard said with exhausted sarcasm.

Marco scaled his cigarette into a brass cuspidor by the desk. His lips quirked grimly. "My holiday greetings, eh? While Denis Blaine gets condolences in the death house for Christmas and *rigor mortis* for New Year's."

"Blaine hasn't gone to trial yet," Brainard reminded him.

"He will in a few days."

Brainard leaned across the desk. "Smith, I've got absolutely no personal grudge against Denis Blaine. It's just that no valid evidence has come forward to prove that Fuchs—and Rohlwing, if they really are the same person—covers an identity as an ex-Nazi."

"He was in my hands!" Marco said, facing the window. "I fouled it, let him escape."

"We should have a report before too—"

Brainard sliced off his words and speared the telephone receiver as the bell emitted a shrill clang. "Both? All right, that I expected. No, keep a routine search under way for Tolenado, but step up the pressure on Rohlwing. We have homicide to contend with there. Yeah, check back regularly."

As the receiver thudded down, Marco asked, "No trace of either one?"

"That's right."

Marco hoisted his glen plaid overcoat from a chair.

"Are you still blank on why Tolenado tried to gun you?" Brainard asked.

"Absolutely," Marco replied with a bland expression.

He had given considerable thought to implicating Vy Cheyney on that score, but had made up his mind against it until he could quiz her on the matter.

"I have to make a check with the photostat office now," the policeman said.

Marco took his cue, ambled toward the door. Brainard raked a hand through his hair and exclaimed: "Blast it, Smith, you look like a man ready to commit suicide. I think your notions are screwy, but there must be one more angle you can try."

Marco pinched the bridge of his nose, wearily. "Where is it? You tell me."

"Well . . . you could at least make a pitch to Comstock, the assistant district attorney handling the Blaine case. Maybe you could persuade Miss Cheyney to sign a statement—secret, of course—setting forth the blackmail plot. That might influence Comstock. Perhaps he could get the commissioner to authorize further investigation. You've jawed at me so long with your notions of ex-Nazis running around loose in the city that I almost believe you."

"Comstock," Marco mused. Then he managed a thin smile. "Worth a try. I'll put you back in the human race, Brainard. Thanks." And he bolted through the door.

Brainard groaned, shrugged into his coat, and snapped out the lights.

Deft hands, pulling and inserting plugs on the

Heinz Brewery switchboard, put the call through immediately.

"Vy? Marco Smith. In thirty minutes, Comstock, the assistant district attorney, is going to grant me a short audience. Yes, the Blaine business. Would you be willing to sign a statement—Comstock'll keep it confidential, of course—about the photostats of that German book shown to you by Nell Bluffton? And the blackmail attempts? I'm running out of rope."

"Where shall I meet you?"

Not over two minutes later, a taxi swung out of the main gate of the Heinz plant. As the car sped through the snowy twilight, Vy gathered her furs closely around her body and closed her eyes for a moment.

Had a voice, simple conversation across distance, ever produced such a peculiar effect before? Yes, once or twice, when she had been younger . . .

How many years had passed since that word had come from her lips? She couldn't recall. With mixed feelings, she formed the letters inaudibly with her mouth, unconsciously giving them an anxious, wondering inflection: *"Love?"*

The fountain pen rasped a signature at the bottom of the hastily typewritten sheet. Vy handed the pen to the official secretary who had transcribed her statement only moments before. Marco leaned against the back of her chair, a thin shine of sweat on his forehead. The secretary vanished, leaving three people in the thickly draped dark-paneled office. Towering up against a mammoth Vidar oil framed on the wall behind him, gray-haired Leland Comstock read the secret deposition without a trace of expression on his face. A clock ticked in the room. Comstock removed a tiny gold key from his watch chain and unlocked the center drawer of his desk. Inserting the deposition in the drawer, he closed the lock and said:

"The paper will be placed in our regular safe tonight, be assured of that, Miss Cheyney."

"Does the theory sound credible?" Marco urged.

Comstock stroked his faintly bluish chin reflectively. "Evidence weighs in your favor, certainly, since Miss Cheyney has been willing to volunteer exceedingly damning information about her firm, for the sake of saving young Blaine. Frankly, the police department and my own investigators presented me with this double-life theory earlier in the case. The appearance of two separate blackmail attempts, each one postulated upon information which would hardly be known to very many people in the U.S.A. but might very well be known—or have been known—to German High Command personnel, strengthens your case."

"What can you do about it?" Marco wanted to know.

"I would be willing to hold off further action

pending a police investigation. If this Fuchs-Rohl-wing person could be unearthed—"

"Will you ask the police commissioner to put more men on it?"

Comstock reddened slightly. "I do not share your complete faith in the theory, Mr. Smith, and therefore I would not want to commit myself to that theory."

Marco protested, "But Brainard said he couldn't act unless you convinced the commissioner. You're just tossing the ball in circles."

Comstock frowned. "Mr. Smith, I appreciate your interest, but I cannot, in effect, grind an ax with the commissioner each time a person comes here to put in a special plea about a single case." Comstock threw a glance at his watch. "If you will both excuse me . . ." He rose.

Marco paced the corridor outside Comstock's office. Vy gripped his arm sympathetically. "I know how you feel," she said. "Everyone except you in this case is only interested in letting someone else stick his neck out."

Marco steered her along the hallway to the elevator. He frowned with concentration, his mind turned inward. Vy could only stand to the side and wish that he might find a path out of the blind maze which seemed to surround him more deeply every moment. "Let me find a taxi for you," Marco muttered as the elevator glided downward. When they reached the street, he handed her into a waiting cab and said, "Thanks. I'll be phoning you tonight or tomorrow. Perhaps we can have dinner—"

"I'd love that," she interrupted.

"Some questions I need to have answered," he went on, almost as if he had not heard her. He closed the taxi door. As the vehicle slid past him, Vy watched through the rear window. Head up, he threaded his way through the crowds. A half-hypnotized expression clouded his face. He'll tear himself to pieces if he doesn't succeed, Vy thought with a sudden chill. Sadness filled her heart as the figure of Marco Polo Smith disappeared behind a drifting curtain of wet, dismal snow.

Brainard telephoned Marco at ten-forty that evening, having just come from the commissioner's home.

Marco listened to Brainard announce wearily: "The commissioner said no."

"Did he offer a reason?"

"He asked me to visualize what would happen if a police officer walked into the home of a wealthy citizen and began making inquiries about possible pro-Nazi sympathies during World War Two." Brainard's voice sounded heavy. "I never had time to think up an answer. He practically booted me out."

"I'm sorry," Marco said.

"He has a short temper, but he cools fast. Don't

worry. His point was sound, though. We would be fools making such inquiries. Look, Smith. Blaine is heading for the electric chair and it can't be stopped. Will you forget the case?"

"You tried, Brainard. I appreciate that."

"Answer my question. Will you forget the case?"

"I wish I could," said Marco, and hung up.

He left the Pacific Minerals Building and returned to his apartment. He stumbled into a thick, nightmare-haunted sleep in which Denis Blaine was electrocuted, revived, strapped in the chair again, electrocuted again, revived again . . . Marco awoke thrashing at the bedclothing, his body running with cold sweat.

# CHAPTER IX

Through the smoke-ridden air of the Heidelberg Lager board of directors' room a wide blade of light cut onto a motion-picture screen stretching across one wall. Animated figures, in full color, began to squeak and cavort on the screen as the projector whirred out the latest campaign presentation of Heidelberg Lager's advertising agency. Gregory Thiess occupied his customary chair at the head of the table, and while his tiny blue eyes focused upon the series of animated television spot announcements, his mind roved restlessly, miles away from the stuffy room. The vaguely bored voice of the Heidelberg account executive droned fuzzily at the rear of his thoughts. Whimsical flutes and oboes piped in the film sound track. Thiess clamped his teeth, thinking wildly: Where is Tolenado?

A full day had passed since the shooting in the photographer's shop, an account of which Thiess had read in the previous evening's late edition. Details had been given of the shooting of Caspar Tole-

# THE DEVIL HAS FOUR FACES

nado, a petty criminal, by private detective M. P. Smith, together with information that Tolenado had vanished from the shop immediately prior to the arrival of the police. All night long Thiess had remained awake, listening to the hourly news broadcasts. Finally, at dawn, one program had carried a bulletin stating that the police had been unable to locate either Tolenado or Fritz Rohlwing. Tortured with worry, numb from loss of sleep, Thiess had motored to his office, ordered all visitors barred, and consumed a large quantity of whisky while waiting and hoping for the telephone to ring.

Noon came. Thiess sent his secretary for the early editions of the papers and a sandwich from the company cafeteria.

As the afternoon ticked away Thiess' apprehension mounted. Why hadn't Tolenado reported, telephoned, made some sign? Tolenado need only ask for assistance to receive it. With so much damning information about him in the hands of Tolenado, Thiess would have put forth unlimited effort and nearly unlimited sums of money to rescue the killer from his plight.

When three-thirty arrived, Thiess had been forced to withdraw to the directors' chamber. To have remained away would have focused undue attention on his wrought-up state, he reasoned. Thiess was not aware, however, that nearly every executive gathered at the long table was only too conscious of the harried state of the founder's son.

Perhaps Tolenado was in no physical danger whatever, but had determined to pull a double cross and use what he knew to bleed money from Thiess.

The unctuous voice of the account executive rose in the dark: "And that, gentlemen, concludes our presentation on spot television advertising for the next budget quarter. I trust the presentation meets with your approval."

As the lights came up and the screen rolled out of sight, polite applause rustled around the table. Leonthals, vice-president and director of advertising and marketing, flicked a glance at Thiess, who was vainly trying to recall even a fraction of what had been visible on the screen.

Leonthals said briefly, "Generally, I thought the presentation was excellent, Quimby. I would quarrel with one or two points, but they will require only minor fixes." Quimby, the account man, crossed his gray-flanneled legs and smiled. A murmur of agreement circulated among the other directors.

"What did you think, Greg?" Leonthals inquired.

Thiess stood up, upsetting a pile of papers before him. "The whole thing should be taken back and kicked around a few more times," he muttered.

Leonthals stifled a gasp. Quimby's face fell.

"Try again. New presentation one week from today. I trust you'll excuse me . . ." And Thiess hurried from the room.

He arrived at his office in a cold sweat. He dismissed his secretary and swallowed several fingers of rye whisky. Then he bundled into his overcoat and rang for his limousine. He left the building through his private rear entrance, loath to face any of his underlings. Word would certainly be circulating now—whispers among the executives about Thiess' strange behavior during the session. Oh, Lord! he thought as his limousine bore him out of the city toward his estate. I'll go crazy if I can't find Tolenado.

As darkness settled, Thiess wolfed a gloomy dinner in the ghostly dining room, paid a short visit to his wife Gretta, then, dressed in old clothing, he drove his powder-blue convertible in to the city. He spent a good part of the night skulking through seamy night spots, making urgent inquiries. These unwholesome haunts had been the home ground of Caspar Tolenado once, when a ten-dollar bill could arrange contact instantly. Now the mere mention of the killer's name produced close-mouthed scowls.

Slightly past four in the morning, when eerie tendrils of mist gripped the highways and the lonely snow-blanketed countryside, Thiess drove back through the gate of his estate, parked his convertible in the drive and staggered upstairs to his room. There he fell into a fitful sleep.

He awoke at ten-thirty with bedclothing wrapped around his neck in a stifling noose. Whimpering and muttering, Thiess staggered to the bathroom. He drew a tub of hot water and stepped down into the sunken tub. The butler knocked discreetly and craned his head around the corner of the door.

"I beg your pardon, Mr. Thiess, but a man is calling on the wire for you. He has been phoning all morning, every fifteen minutes. No, it's not Mr. Southart." The butler's nose wrinkled faintly. "He sounds—well, sir, almost mentally incompetent. Thick, slurred speech, if you understand. Yet he keeps insisting that you will speak with him."

Thiess had been toying with the notion of taking a gun, going directly to Vy and threatening to kill her if she didn't co-operate. The butler's arrival had intruded upon his thoughts, and he asked with a scowl:

"Who the hell is this man?"

"He gave the name of Marvel, sir," replied the butler.

Thiess batted his eyes owlishly. "Marvel? Look here, Perkins! I can't be bothered with crackpot telephone calls. Get rid of him."

"Very well, sir." The butler hesitated. "He did want me to mention, sir, that he wanted to speak with you concerning the National Bank of Stockholm. Does that mean anything to . . . Mr. Thiess!" Perkins rushed forward. "What's wrong, sir? You're white as a sheet!"

"Plug in a telephone! Then get out! Leave me alone!" Thiess roared.

Perkins exited and returned a moment later with a receiver, which he plugged into the wall. Thiess hoisted himself to the edge of the tub. The bathroom door clicked shut. His heart pounded furiously as he spoke into the mouthpiece: "Gregory Thiess talking."

The man calling himself Marvel pronounced his words as if he had been carefully rehearsed. Marvel wished to call on Thiess the following evening concerning deposits made by Thiess with the National Bank of Stockholm during the years 1938 to 1943. Numbly Thiess listened, and let the new horror take possession of his being. When he tried to hang up the receiver it slid from his soapy hand, plunking into the bath water. Beneath the surface of the water, strange squawking noises burbled up along the telephone cord.

Caspar Tolenado, reeling and half out of his mind with pain, had gone to ground in a cheap hotel in the worst section of the city.

At twilight of the snowy night on which Thiess set out on his vain pilgrimage, Tolenado summoned strength enough to point his .45 at the ancient rheumy-eyed bellboy of the Edgarson Hotel. The frightened old man returned with a pimply pharmacist's apprentice from a nearby drugstore. The boy dressed Tolenado's wound, swore in abject terror to reveal nothing, and warned Tolenado that he had better see a doctor. Tolenado waved him out with his gun barrel, locked the flimsy door and lay down on the uncomfortable brass bed, his eyes open, wondering whether he would live or die.

He slept uneasily, fingers curled around his gun. Night came on again. Feverishly Tolenado watched a neon sign outside his window spill red and green light through soiled lace curtains. The sign pulsed on and off like a heartbeat. From the cocktail bar attached to the hotel below rose the thundering strains of a jukebox, as someone played *Perdido* again and again. Down the hall a drunken female laugh shrilled. A man cursed on the other side of the tissue-thin walls. Tolenado slept, wakened and slept again, pain like a firebrand in his chest.

The frantic juke music blasted his tiny room all night long, but in the morning he was able to stagget out to a restaurant for a cup of coffee and a sweet roll. Clutching his overcoat to conceal his blood-stained shirt, he returned to the hotel and slept again, the .45 on his chest, blood pumping slowly as he fought his strange battle for life.

One by one, each of the visitors had been escorted by taciturn police guards to Denis Blaine's cell. First, Karl Strauss, then Denis' lawyer, next Diana Meadows, and last, Marco Smith.

The lawyer departed hastily after refusing to comment on prospects for victory in the case. Now, old Strauss and his niece Diana waited on a wooden bench in the white-walled antechamber for the detective to emerge. Sounds rang hollowly. A white tile floor and fluorescent ceiling fixtures lent a mood of somber sterility to the antechamber.

Karl Strauss, bundled in a heavy black suit, blinked at the young girl beside him. All traces of joviality had disappeared from his face.

Diana watched him pityingly. He had engaged the best lawyer available, staked a vast sum of money on freeing Denis, and was finding his efforts thwarted. At one point, Diana had suggested, in a fit of fear, that he employ his fortune to bring judicious pressure on certain important officials involved in the case.

Strauss had purpled and delivered a tight-lipped tirade on an immigrant's respect for the justice of the American judicial system. With blind faith, Strauss believed that the problem would unravel itself, and his unswerving support of a scrupulously honest defense for Denis made her feel cheap and shabby for having made the suggestion to the proud old man.

Marco Smith emerged from behind the ponderous steel door, and Diana rushed forward. "Did— did you think of something?"

Marco's smile was thin. "No, nothing. Denis wanted the explanation of Cagliostro's bullet trick that I gave to you earlier today. I pointed out how the stunt could have worked," Marco said sourly, "if Fuchs was actually Fuchs-Ohm. I'm beginning to doubt it myself."

Strauss seized the detective's arm. "You must not doubt, Mr. Smith. You must press on, unearth new evidence."

Marco walked with his companions toward the street entrance.

"With the trial beginning in forty-eight hours? What chance have I got to locate the man who calls himself Rohlwing?"

They moved into the slushy grayness of the street outside. Traffic hooted. Light mist obscured the air, and the world had a soiled, unfriendly gray cast.

"So far, I've failed," Marco said softly. He wrenched each word from his lips as though it caused pain. "I don't approve of wearing sackcloth in public, mind you, or of rationalizing failure. This little speech is simply stating the facts, because we had all better prepare for the worst." Marco paused, then spoke with even greater bitterness. "You've wasted your money, I think."

Diana shook her head. "You've tried hard, Mr. Smith. You risked death to trace the photographer, and Vy Cheyney, from your story, put herself in a terribly compromising situation to help Denis. That none of it has been successful we can cross off to chance—bad luck . . ." Her eyes darkened. "The workings of an evil world, perhaps."

Deep in his black overcoat, Karl Strauss rumbled, "Yah, we are human beings only. What else could you have done, Mr. Smith?"

"Caught the man we want." Marco stuffed his

hands in his pockets, turned on his heel, and with a curt syllable of farewell stalked away in the crowd. Diana watched his dejected figure retreat through the murk.

Marco lifted several unimportant letters and circulars off the floor beneath the mail slot and tossed them lackadaisically onto his desk. From a drawer, he produced the list of leading city families with German blood in their backgrounds. As he went over the names, however, the typewriting blurred together and the words became meaningless. He pushed the list aside and lit a cigarette.

Three seconds later, he lit another. He tore the wrapping from a new book, took a cursory glance at the foreword and table of contents, and then slipped the volume out of sight in a lower drawer. The building elevator whined in the distance. His cubicle smelled of last night's sweeping compound.

Glancing at his watch, he decided to check his answering service. It reported that Assistant District Attorney Leland Comstock had telephoned shortly past lunchtime, had requested him to call back. Marco squinted through cigarette smoke and speared the phone dial. Comstock's secretary put Marco's call through.

"Marco Smith, Comstock."

"Yes, Smith. I recalled our conversation of a few days ago when I heard this morning via the grapevine that the police commissioner had refused to investigate the Blaine affair along the lines you indicated. That's unfortunate. I recognized that you were firmly convinced of the truth of your beliefs."

"Reasonably certain."

"You understand, of course, that I still can't afford to jeopardize my position by openly supporting your theories. If I intimated that certain well-known families in our city had Nazi sympathizers in their ranks, it would be sheer political dynamite." Marco said nothing. "Thus I can't exert pressure on the commissioner. But privately I can grant you more time to carry out your own investigations, if you're still interested. Would that be agreeable, Smith? A private understanding between us?"

"Would it!" Marco nearly shouted.

"Very well." Comstock cleared his throat. "Blaine's trial is docketed to start two days hence. It's possible for me to delay it an additional two days."

"Only two days? That's not—"

"Good Lord, man, it's forty-eight hours more than you have this instant!" Comstock shouted.

Marco backed off. "You're right. Four days it is. Thank you, Mr. Comstock. If Denis Blaine is freed, he'll want to know you helped him."

"He mustn't know!" Comstock cautioned sternly. "This stay can be accomplished only through manipulations of a delicate sort. Should they become public, it would be unpleasant for me. I simply do it because—well—" Comstock chuckled, puzzled. "Frankly, I can't say exactly why, since I can't rationally believe your theories."

"I understand, sir. And thanks again."

"Very well, Smith. You won't hear from me again. Four days from now, Denis Blaine goes to trial. That is all I can do. Goodbye, Smith."

"Goodbye, Mr. Comstock."

Marco swiveled his chair around to regard the mist-laden panorama of the city. Out there, Rohlwing waited. Out there, the killer was hidden—the killer: Rohlwing—Fuchs—Fuchs-Ohm, butcher of Nell Bluffton. Marco's eyes went hard.

Four days.

Four days to save a man from the electric chair.

## CHAPTER X

At the same hour in which Marco Smith received his temporary reprieve from Assistant District Attorney Comstock, an exceptionally tall man scuttled into the doorway of a dusty-looking shop in the city's Bohemian district. Antique books and stacks of tattered back-date magazines filled the windows, which bore chipped gilt letters announcing: WAGNER ULM, USED BOOK AND MAGAZINE DEALER.

The tall man unlocked the door and entered the shop. He flicked on overhead lights which illuminated a small room whose walls bulged with bookcases containing used volumes and magazines of every description. The tall man rolled up a green blind which had masked the door and peeled off a crudely lettered cardboard sign affixed to the glass. The sign said, *Closed for Vacation*.

Taking hardly a glance at the stocks of reading material, the man moved to a rear room. There, in the light of a tin-shaded bulb suspended from the

## THE DEVIL HAS FOUR FACES

ceiling, he inspected himself in a cracked mirror hanging askew on one wall.

He inclined his head this way and that, studying his image. Elevator shoes added perceptibly to his height. His stomach bulged prominently beneath a threadbare brown suit, but one of the straps chafed his shoulder. Unbuttoning his shirt, he remedied the difficulty, so that the padding fitted comfortably around his middle. He rumpled his gray hair slightly, then stepped to a small iron safe in one corner. He spun the dial and removed a small medicine-dropper bottle and a little cardboard box. Tilting his head back, he droppered liquid into the corners of his eyes. He opened the box, and in a twinkling a pair of contact lenses had changed his eyes from blue to brown.

A chuckle of satisfaction escaped his lips. He examined a heavy gold watch. He had arrived just in time. Marvel would show up at any moment.

Meanwhile, Wagner Ulm occupied himself with an inspection of the rear room. In one corner stood an object which brought an exclamation of pleasure to his lips. Upon a platform, which stood on casters some twelve inches from the floor, rested a square unpainted wooden box large enough to accommodate a human being crouched inside it. The contraption had a hinged top and twelve slots at various positions on each side.

Ulm lifted the lid and whistled appreciatively at the cleverly concealed hiding space beneath the top section. So . . . his friend had been indulging his hobby and completing a sword cabinet at the time of his death, eh? Ulm chuckled. Very well, the magic illusion would give him a project on which to exercise his own skill. He would complete it and thus pass the time until the final coup was completed. He had been worrying too much of late, probably as a result of the narrow squeak at the photographer's quarters. That damned detective, Marco Polo Smith, had been making it hot for him. Lucky that the three blinds—the magic shop of Fuchs, the photo studio of Rohlwing, the bookshop of Ulm—had all been set up carefully in advance, so that a switch in personalities could be completed in an hour's time.

Thinking of Marco Smith brought ugly lines to the face of Wagner Ulm. While taking the streetcar to his new headquarters, Ulm had mulled over the problem of the detective and come to a decision. At the earliest possible instant, he was going to murder Marco Polo Smith.

Ulm's thoughts of homicide were diverted by the discovery of a number of cans of bright-colored lacquer and several brushes piled against the wall behind the unfinished sword cabinet. Also, he unearthed a collection of sharp-pointed, keenly-honed sabers wrapped in newspaper, two dozen in all. He lifted one of the weapons and cut a few experimental swaths through the air. Then he tested the blade with the ball of his thumb. A tiny line of blood appeared.

Ulm inserted the saber in one of the openings in the side of the cabinet, rammed it home with force. The point shot out through the corresponding slot on the opposite side. Ulm hefted another saber and jammed it through the box. What pleasure it would be to have Smith crouching inside the locked case!

He returned to the front of the store in time to see a massive, almost inhuman figure duck its misshapen head beneath the top of the doorframe and enter, blinking and peering around like a child.

"Good afternoon, Marvel," Ulm called. "Come this way, into the rear."

The gigantic figure shambled forward. He presented a spectacular sight, towering well over six feet, with huge shoulders and long arms with hamlike hands hanging nearly to his knees. Thick lips, a broken nose, and scar tissue about his ears and tiny eyes declared him a piece of refuse from the fight game. Actually he had drifted from boxing into wrestling, until his brains had become too mangled even for that carefully contrived sport. Brute power and rudimentary understanding were all that remained. He did not even know his own name. Once, he remembered, he had been billed as The Masked Marvel, and thus he picked the word to identify himself in the strange half-world of skid-row derelicts in which he lived.

Patting Marvel's arm in friendly fashion, Ulm said approvingly, "You are right on time, Marvel. Excellent. I appreciate loyalty."

Marvel licked his lips. "You helped me. You picked me up in that flop. You pay me. You treat me okay."

Ulm removed several sheets of paper from his pocket. Photostats. He unrolled them and pressed them into the giant's hand. Marvel peered at the papers owlishly and scratched his greasy cap, puzzled.

Ulm guided Marvel's hand, inserting the papers inside the man's worn overcoat.

"Do you remember the man Thiess you called on the telephone yesterday?" Marvel nodded in response. "Tonight you must visit him. He is expecting you. I will locate a taxi for you, and give the driver instructions. Say nothing to the driver, or anyone—except Thiess. Do you understand that, Marvel?"

"Yes, I do," was all the giant could reply, nodding his head dumbly.

"Show the papers I gave you—to Thiess."

"These papers?" Marvel inquired, producing the photostats again.

Ulm stifled his impatience. "That's correct, yes. Now put them away. Don't lose them. Do not leave Mr. Thiess' home until he gives you two thousand . . ." Ulm hesitated. "No, make it three thousand. In cash. And understand this very clearly,

## THE DEVIL HAS FOUR FACES

Marvel." Ulm stressed each word. "You are not to leave Thiess until he puts in your hand three thousand dollars in cash. Tell him you will return in one week for the same amount. If he should try to detain you—"

Marvel's gnarled brow wrinkled. He rolled the word on his tongue, vaguely: "De-tain?"

"Stop you, prevent you from leaving. You know what to do?"

At last, the true nature of the pitiful giant became apparent. He lifted his huge hands before his face, and made a series of grotesque twisting motions. A thick-witted smile contorted his lips. Ulm matched the giant's smile with one of satisfaction. "Fine, fine. When you return I'll have ten dollars waiting for you."

"Ten dollars," Marvel echoed. "You good to me, Mr. Ulm."

Ulm led the giant to the street. He slipped into his overcoat and left the shop untended for a moment while he accompanied Marvel to the corner. As they walked through the mist, Ulm inquired, "Marvel, would you kill a man for me, if that became necessary? Have I treated you well—well enough so you would kill?"

"Tell me who I got to kill, Mr. Ulm," Marvel replied with fervor.

"No one, at the present," Ulm said with a laugh. "I was just making sure, that's all."

He hailed a taxi and told the driver: "This man

is delivering a book for me." He gave the driver the address of Thiess' estate and pressed a number of bills into his hand. "Take him there, wait, and bring him back." The cabby agreed, gears clashed and the taxi shot away. Ulm strolled back to the shop.

In the rear of his shop he procured a Luger, which he deposited in his coat. He extinguished the lights, locked up and left. His watch told him the time was four-thirty. He signaled a taxi and instructed the driver to take him to the Pacific Minerals Building.

Marco Smith turned up the collar of his coat and swept through the revolving doors of the Pacific Minerals Building at ten past five. He slogged along through the mist-laden afternoon, crowds jostling him at every turn. He did not see the tall, stout, brown-eyed man who followed half a block behind.

Muted violins set the air humming with a slow, bittersweet refrain. The black-jacketed waiter seated Vy Cheyney at the gleaming table where thick golden candles cast warm highlights on her auburn hair. Marco listened a moment longer to the haunting melody, then took his chair. "That's called *He Was Too Good to Me*. Do you know it?" Her gesture indicated she did not. "It's Rodgers and Hart. Not played often. Sometimes I wonder why people are foolish enough to forget songs like that."

Vy treated him to a warm smile. "You are an amazing man, Mr. Smith. I—" Sudden embarrassment caught her and she averted her gaze.

Marco gave a gentle chuckle. "No. I'm a walking encyclopedia of useless facts. My avocation is history of all sorts—political, literary, social—and no one pays any attention to those things any more." He lit a pair of cigarettes, passed one to her, and studied her face across the circle of candlelight. In utter seriousness, he said, "You are lovely tonight."

"Wonderful!" she said with light mockery. "The prettier the girl, the better the meal the gentleman is willing to buy." She picked up a huge gold-embossed menu. "Let's order a cocktail and dinner before we break out that list you mentioned. I know how important Denis Blaine's case is, but . . ." Again an electric spark flamed within her eyes as their gazes met. She moistened her lips slightly. ". . . but this is too nice to spoil."

And so it was. Marco let his senses revel in the comfortable surroundings and the beauty of the young woman across the table from him. The French Pheasant was the finest restaurant in the city, a great high-ceilinged Victorian room with velvet hangings on the walls and candles on all the tables.

They drank a martini apiece, and then dined on superb whole lobster. A jot of Drambuie completed Marco's meal. He sat back in his chair and lighted a cigar, wondering how the time had passed so swiftly. He was acutely aware of the foolish pretense of his ambition. That a young, beautiful, and wealthy woman should bother with a man engaged in what was generally regarded as a rather shoddy profession was a notion too outlandish to entertain long.

He pulled out the typewritten list. "I suppose we ought to give it a try." He explained his plan, telling her that the list had been made up by Karl Strauss. Vy examined it for several minutes. While she did so, Marco was half-aware that a waiter had seated someone on the opposite side of a pillar next to Vy.

"Schoenhorn . . . Kruger . . . Horst . . ." Vy read the names aloud, softly. "All very respectable families, Marco. But there is one man on the list who falls into a category with Andrew Strauss and my late husband." A touch of bitterness clouded her eyes. Vy's red-tipped nail indicated a typewritten line. "Gregory Thiess, of Heidelberg Lager."

"You think he might be the next victim?"

"If he hasn't been contacted already, I'd be very much surprised."

"Do you know him? Or are you guessing?"

"I know him."

Marco frowned. "That bitterness in your voice isn't becoming. Or like you."

"No?" She tapped her cigarette nervously in a tray, and sipped her brandy. "I hope you're not putting me on a pedestal, Marco—"

"Close to it. Very close."

"Because," she hurried on, "you'd be terribly

## THE DEVIL HAS FOUR FACES

disappointed. Every man and woman, I suspect, has something hidden in their make-up. You wouldn't care to hear about my connection with Gregory Thiess. It's a nasty story, almost a true confession. And I like you too much to let you know what I really am."

"Be serious," Marco said. "You have no reason to talk that way."

"But I do."

Marco hesitated. He rolled his cigar between his fingers for a moment. "Have you any solid basis for believing that Thiess might ever have contributed to the Nazi cause?"

"Yes. He told me straight out one time that he sympathized with Hitler." Her mouth wrinkled distastefully. "He believed Hitler had the right idea when he used the gas ovens. Greg is a nasty person, Marco. I realize it more fully since—" She paused, then forced herself to continue: "I was once in love with him. I had an affair with him, in fact. He . . ." Down went her voice. She studied the gleaming tablecloth self-consciously, and her face flushed. "Gregory Thiess fathered a child of mine, Marco. A little girl. She's in an orphanage. I pay for her support. She's a wonderful child—" Vy's eyes brimmed with tears. "I've never told anyone else before. Do you despise me?"

Marco shook his head. "Were you in love with Thiess?"

"I thought so. I was lonely. I met Greg Thiess

through business channels. It was a brief affair; even as it was just beginning, I sensed what sort of a person he really was. By the time Virginia was born, we had broken it off completely. He contributed part of her support for a time, after my husband died, then let me take the whole burden. Not that I mind," she added hastily. "The—the fact that I have never acknowledged her is the bitterest part of all. I'm weak, Marco." She shuddered slightly. "I see my daughter now as a very terrible skeleton."

"You say she's in an orphanage," Marco asked. "Near here?"

"Just outside—" Vy looked up as the waiter hesitated tactfully near their table. Marco waved for more drinks. When the waiter retired Vy smiled wanly.

"Vy, I'm glad you told me."

"Why?"

Marco took her hand across the table. Her skin, warm, faintly perfumed, tingled against his palm. "Because at this moment, watching you, seeing your beauty, I have all sorts of wild notions about *us*. At least in my woolgathering, things seem to work out for us."

"Work out? You mean . . ."

Marco nodded. "The moth-eaten story about the poor boy and the rich girl. I feel cheated. On the screen it always ends happily; with us, it can't. The wound feels pretty raw."

"Are you positive it can't?" Vy asked.

Marco's lips narrowed to a thin line. "Don't be a fool. You run a million-dollar corporation. I run a two-bit detective agency. I could never leave my work. Neither could you."

"Your appraisal is pitifully correct, Marco," she said sadly. "I'm too spineless to desert the money now. I saw my parents slave on a dirt farm in poverty, and all my life I've been trying to wash the dirt out of my pores. Money helps. Give it up? I couldn't. At least—" She pressed one hand to her forehead. "If I could only straighten out the tangle of my own thoughts, then, perhaps . . ."

The violins soared and pulsed away. A waiter passed carrying a drink to the diner behind the pillar at Vy's back, but Marco paid no attention. Vy drained her brandy.

Marco frowned at the smoke rising from his cigar. Vy had to speak twice before he heard.

"I had an ulterior motive when you asked me to dinner this evening."

"Oh?"

"Marco, I'm desperately afraid for Virginia. I want to take her from the orphanage temporarily, to guard her."

A new thought struck the detective. "Would your daughter have anything to do with Tolenado's threats, that day in your apartment? And with his insistence that you 'agree' to something?"

"It would. Greg wants to take custody of Virginia,

legally but not publicly. I turned him down flat."

"What reason does he have for wanting custody?"

"Lord only knows. I couldn't comprehend all his chatter. He said he was teetering on the edge of financial ruin, and that only by putting certain holdings in Virginia's name could he avert the collapse. I told him to get out. Then he sent Tolenado to threaten me. I'm afraid he might try something like kidnapping."

"He could spend the rest of his life in prison for that," Marco said.

"From the way he talked when he made his original proposal, if he doesn't get custody of Virginia, things will be even worse. Marco, I know Greg too well. He's a vicious opportunist. He drove his own wife almost insane with his philandering. He's pulled hundreds of shady deals. And when a person gets in his way, he uses an ax. If he needed Virginia, I'm sure he would stop at nothing to get her."

Marco's brows furrowed. "You want me to take Virginia from the orphanage and watch out for her until this blows over?"

"I know it's unfair, but she's my own flesh and blood. Weak as I am, I don't want anything to happen to her."

"This explains Tolenado," Marco said. "I'll bet he reported to Thiess that you'd hired a detective. Thus the attempt to kill me. Does Thiess know the orphanage where Virginia is staying?"

"Of course."

"Um. That's not so good."

"Marco . . ."

"What?"

"Will you help?"

"For you?"

Vy touched his hand again. "Shall I tell you what I'm thinking at this moment, Marco?"

"Go on."

"I'm thinking I love you. I'm thinking I've fallen genuinely in love for the first time in my whole messed-up, miserable life. And knowing that you're the right man, the best one that ever came along, I haven't the courage to say to myself, 'Vy, you're finished with Heinz Beer and annual reports and earnings statements and sales promotion campaigns and all the rest.' I like the money—the dividend checks four times a year from my husband's preferred stock. A lovely green noose of dollar bills around my neck, and I can't cut it. I want to—desperately—because of you. But I . . ." She struggled to continue, and could not.

"That's all right," Marco said quietly. He forced a smile to his lips. "We'll cross it off as one of those trips to the moon, as the song goes." He summoned the waiter and paid the check. "Shall we go?"

They drove through the night mist to the Edinburgh Arms. Parking half a block from the building entrance, Marco said, "Telephone the orphanage in the morning and tell them I'm to pick up Virginia. By the way—does she go under your name?"

"No. She's called Virginia Brown."

"I've got some friends—a newspaper reporter and his wife . . . They've always wanted a family. They'd give anything to take care of a little girl, even for a few days. She'll be safe with them." He opened the car door. "You forgot to tell me the name of the orphanage."

"The Orphanage of Saint Boniface," she said softly.

They strolled toward the lighted portico of the luxurious building. Vy slipped her arm into his and rested her head on his shoulder as they rode up in the elevator. She unlocked the door and turned and whispered softly, "I . . . could ask you to come inside. But if it ever works out for us, darling, I want it to be a hundred percent right and honest, from the very beginning."

Marco bent forward and kissed her on the lips, straightened abruptly and headed for the elevator.

She watched him as he entered the elevator and disappeared from sight. By the time she closed the door to her apartment, she was crying.

"Check, waiter! And hurry!"

Seated at the small table behind the pillar where Vy and Marco Polo Smith had dined, a stout, brown-eyed man paid his bill. The gold candle on

# THE DEVIL HAS FOUR FACES

his table threw weird, twisted gleams on his lined face. The man calling himself Wagner Ulm had overheard every word passing between the woman and the detective. His eyes gleamed as he threaded his way out of the fashionable restaurant.

"So," he said to himself, shouldering into the mist, "there is a child . . ."

# CHAPTER XI

The hours were dropping away toward dawn when the tall figure of the bogus bookseller slouched through the bistros and strip-and-clip clubs on the edge of the underworld. Ulm had offered bribes for information at first, and received blank stares in return from bartenders and percentage girls. After midnight passed, he began to grow more desperate.

In the nervous, shifty expressions, Ulm had glimpsed knowledge quickly masked, truth turned into a lie. Therefore he abandoned his wallet for his Luger.

One plaid-jacketed waiter gasped in alarm as he felt the Luger's cold muzzle grind against his thigh beneath a table. He advised Ulm to visit a strip club called the Tick-Tock. Ulm drove recklessly to the run-down section. One o'clock was fifteen minutes gone . . .

At the Tick-Tock hot trumpets brayed under a low ceiling and groups of sailors lined the orange-spotlighted bar where a girl performed a dance

# THE DEVIL HAS FOUR FACES

with a feather boa. Ulm's brown eyes, shining with a moist film, spotted a rear curtained entrance. He turned to the bartender. "Where may I find a Miss Bea Simmonds?"

"That's her grinding away on the stage," replied the perspiring bartender.

Ulm slipped through the curtain and stood in a dim alcove off the rancid hallway at the rear of the club. Presently high heels clicked a sharp tattoo, and the curtains parted. Ulm stepped out. "Excuse me—are you Miss Simmonds?"

"That's right. I'm Bea Simmonds."

"I've been told that you might help me find Caspar Tolenado."

Bea Simmonds tried to lie: "Tolenado? I never heard of any guy named—"

Ulm cut her off harshly. "Are you not one of his women?"

"Listen, mister, I . . ." She passed a hand across her dripping forehead.

Ulm withdrew his Luger and pushed it forward until the muzzle rested along her rather thin ribs. "Where is Tolenado?"

"Ed—Edgarson Hotel," Bea Simmonds stammered. "Three blocks over, on Greener Street. Only, I'm not sure he's there any longer!" she protested, terrified. "He came in to see me last night looking pretty shaky . . . Take that gun away!" Her voice wavered on the edge of hysteria. "And—stop—stop staring at me." She cowered against the wall.

Ulm put his gun out of sight and melted into the shadows. Moments later the metal door leading to the alley gave a soft clang. Bea Simmonds trembled against the wall and wondered why she had been so utterly terrified.

His eyes, she thought. Those brown eyes, knowing, laughing, cruel.

All his senses responding with a gunman's instant alertness to danger, Caspar Tolenado leaped lightly out of bed at the soft rapping on the door. Through the tattered lace curtains of the cheap hotel room, red and green neon light washed his face with sickly hues as he fastened a firm grip on the butt of his .45 and padded toward the door. He listened for a moment and heard only light breathing. He called:

"Who's there?"

"Tolenado?"

"Wrong room. Get the hell away and let me sleep." Tolenado bit his lip. The exertion of leaping from the bed so quickly had sent new pain coursing through his body. He clasped the door handle for support.

"Let me in, Tolenado! My name is Wagner Ulm. I want to pay you a thousand dollars cash for information. Don't be a fool, man!" the voice urged. "Open the door."

Tolenado clenched his teeth. "I never heard of

## THE DEVIL HAS FOUR FACES 171

you." His mind purred a warning that the caller might be a detective. Abruptly, however, he realized that he could not flee in his weakened condition, so that nothing would be lost if the caller proved legitimate. "If you really mean it about the thousand, slip the money under the door. As much as you have. Then we'll see."

Angry mutterings sounded from the opposite side of the panel. A thick packet of bills popped through the crack below the door. Tolenado limped to the window and counted the roll by the pulsing neon's glow. One thousand dollars, right enough, in twenty-dollar bills. He rallied his strength and threw off the safety chain. It took all his effort to stuff the money into his grimy shirt pocket and stagger back to the bed. The visitor drew the shade and snapped on the overhead light.

Tolenado had collapsed on the bed, groaning. Now he threw an arm across his forehead to shield his eyes from the glare. He squinted at Ulm, whom he had never seen before. He still kept his .45 in his fist, but his grip grew less secure by the moment. Wagner Ulm seemed to tower to the ceiling, a gigantic figure whose face was a smeary white blur.

"All I wish to learn," Ulm said softly, "is the name and location of the orphanage in which the child Virginia Brown is kept."

"Who—" Tolenado's words were punctuated by

a fit of coughing. He grasped the bedframe for support. "Who are you working for?" he managed to croak at last.

"No one."

"What makes you think—"

"Please, Mr. Tolenado. It's three o'clock, and speed is imperative. The name of the orphanage, in exchange for the one thousand dollars."

Tolenado wanted only to return to the soothing dark, where he could sleep and forget his aching body. "Saint Boniface," he wheezed. "The Orphanage of Saint Boniface. You take the Inter-City Turnpike for eight miles . . ."

At the conclusion of directions, the stranger put out the overhead light and rolled up the shade. Through slitted eyes Tolenado saw the tall stranger bend forward, limned suddenly in a spurt of red neon. A nightmarish face peered down. "Good night, Mr. Tolenado," cooed the remote voice. "My exceeding thanks for your assistance." A dark shape bulked in Tolenado's vision. Too late, he realized it was a thick pillow being clamped down over his face. He sent out frantic commands to his hand, but the .45 had already been knocked clear. The pillow obliterated all sound.

Ulm's hand inserted a weapon into the folds of the pillow, jammed it downward and blew a hole in Tolenado's face.

No one in the Edgarson Hotel heard the muffled report. In less than sixty seconds the figure of Wag-

# THE DEVIL HAS FOUR FACES

ner Ulm had blended into the mist on the street outside. Caspar Tolenado lay sprawled on the brass bed, a bloody pillow beside him.

Across an expanse of sodden ground Ulm could see several brick buildings crowded together. In the east, pale light struggled through the mist. Ulm glanced over his shoulder to make certain he had concealed his automobile well enough on the shoulder of the little-used road. Then he jumped, caught the top crossbar of the iron fence, pulled himself upward and dropped with a heavy squish onto the wet turf inside the grounds. He ran across the lawn, up to the darkened buildings of the Orphanage of St. Boniface, moving with surprising agility. The elaborate padded stomach had been left behind.

At one corner of a single-story building a service light cast a wide area of ground into sharp relief. Ulm avoided this. Through the stillness of the night a bell in the chapel tower began to toll the hour of five. Ulm stole along the face of the low building, peered in several windows and decided the structure was a storage facility. Behind this, he found a three-storied high-windowed building with fire escapes zigzagging up the sides.

Through one window he glimpsed the face of a small boy asleep in a wooden bunk. At one end of the building he located an unlocked door. Quietly he stole inside and down the aisles between the sleeping children.

Sister Carmen entered the first-floor dormitory on her usual early morning rounds at six-thirty. Gray, chilly light fell through the tall leaded windows of the converted estate building. Sister Carmen smiled gently. The first floor housed the younger children and it always gave her a thrill of quiet pleasure to gaze down on their untroubled sleeping faces.

As the kindly faced middle-aged nun studied the long room, two things caught her eye and filled her with alarm: a pair of mussed, empty beds halfway down the aisle, and the figure of a small boy crouching in a far corner.

Sister Carmen hurried forward. The boy's sobbing became audible as she drew closer. He huddled in the corner as if seeking protection from some awful horror. His nightshirt was twisted over his slender legs, his fists pressed to his eyes.

Sister Carmen knelt down. "Jamie," she said softly.

Jamie's eyes flew wide and he would have uttered a scream had not Sister Carmen touched gentle fingers to his lips. In a moment the boy recognized her as a friend, and wrapped his hands protectively in the folds of her habit.

"A big thing woke me in the dark," the boy sobbed. "Whispering at me, whispering and whispering, wanting to know where Virginia Brown was asleep, so I said over there, and pointed. Then I ran down here. The thing whispered at me some more, told me not to cry, or awful things would happen. I saw it, with a hand across Virginia's mouth. It carried her . . ." The boy's lips trembled and he closed his eyes again.

"Jamie," Sister Carmen urged softly, "you must tell me more. Where did this man take Virginia?"

"It wasn't a man," the boy insisted. "It was big, a big tall thing with a voice that made me cry. It touched me. Its—its hands were cold and wet—"

"Where is Virginia, Jamie?" the nun asked, beginning to panic.

"It carried her through the door. There." And he pointed to the door at the opposite end.

Dread mounted in Sister Carmen's heart. She summoned another nun to care for the boy, then hurried through the indicated door into the chill dawn. Large, deeply indented footsteps stood out clearly on the soft ground, leading in a line toward the fence which bordered the road. By the time Sister Carmen returned from the fence, she knew the truth: Virginia Brown had been kidnapped.

The telephone awoke Marco Smith at three minutes past seven. He rolled over and smothered his head with the blanket. The phone continued ringing. Marco untangled himself from the covers and shuffled across the bedroom into the small living room of his bachelor apartment and collapsed into a chair beside a massive mahogany console. Lifting the lid, he pulled the telephone out of the record storage section and lifted the receiver. From the opposite wall a brooding African mask of ebony leered at him.

He yawned into the receiver. "Hullo?"

A stream of disconnected words burst from the wire. His sleepy air vanished and he sat bolt upright. Vy Cheyney, barely able to talk, managed to communicate only a portion of her message. Marco cut her off:

"Hold on a second, Vy! Hold it! Slow down! . . . Now what about Virginia? You say she disappeared from the orphanage last night?"

"Early this—this morning," Vy replied. Her wild sobbing subsided briefly. Marco lit a cigarette and sucked smoke deep into his lungs. Vy said, "When Sister Carmen went into the dormitory at six-thirty, she discovered Virginia was gone. She telephoned me just a moment ago. I begged her not to notify the police until I talked with you."

"Good move," Marco said. "Is Sister Carmen certain Virginia has been kidnapped? I mean, could there be a chance that Virginia wandered off to another part of the orphanage during the night and hasn't been located yet? Has she checked on it?"

"Virginia was kidnapped. Sister Carmen followed a set of tracks from the dormitory to a high fence that separates the orphanage grounds from the road. Someone entered the dormitory during the night. A —a little boy named Jamie was awakened by what he called a—a 'thing that whispered.'" Hearing

# THE DEVIL HAS FOUR FACES

the anguish in Vy's voice, Marco could visualize the shudder that shook her when she described the unknown kidnapper. "This—thing," Vy struggled on, "asked the boy where Virginia slept, which bed was hers. Then Jamie hid, but he saw this person carry Virginia from the dormitory. The boy was too terrified to make an outcry." Vy's voice filled with new horror: "Marco, Greg must have sent someone there last night . . . someone who only had to walk in and walk out. Taking my daughter."

"An orphanage is no prison," Marco said. "You can hardly expect them to be prepared for kidnapping of children that people supposedly care nothing about."

"I acted very badly with Sister Carmen, I know. But Virginia is— Oh, Marco—Virginia! If Greg hurts her—"

"Control yourself!" Marco said harshly. "I know you're upset. But it doesn't help to get hysterical. Do you really think Thiess engineered the kidnapping?"

"Who else would have any reason?"

Marco nodded. "Then Sister Carmen must call the police. But maybe I can persuade her to withhold certain information."

"Are the police necessary, Marco?"

"If I can't locate Virginia in one or two hours, then all the help available will be needed. Let me handle that end, darling. You try to stay calm. Drink some coffee. Turn on the radio, listen to music, anything. Just don't think too much about what's happened."

Vy persisted: "The police could very well focus too much attention on the case. If Greg—"

"Leave it to me."

"To think that Virginia's in the hands of that beast Tolenado."

"Yes, he probably pulled the snatch right enough. Now let me hang up. Remember what I said—keep calm. Stick close to your phone. As soon as I have any information, I'll ring, but don't go off the deep end if you hear nothing from me for a few hours. Agreed?"

All that Vy Cheyney could say was: "I'll try, Marco."

"Okay, darling. Hang on." He jammed the receiver onto the cradle and sprinted toward the bedroom.

Marco Smith's face assumed a hardened cast as he pulled on his trousers and knotted his tie. He threw coffee into the percolator and returned to the telephone while the coffee-maker began to bubble. Marco dialed the Orphanage of St. Boniface and had Sister Carmen called to the wire. When he identified himself, the nun said:

"Oh, yes, Mr. Smith. Miss Cheyney told me you would be calling. You can't begin to know how deeply shocked I am by this awful thing."

# THE DEVIL HAS FOUR FACES 179

"I understand your feelings, Sister," Marco said. "You haven't called the police yet, have you?"

"No. Miss Cheyney requested that I not telephone them until after I spoke with you. Since she is Virginia's guardian, I complied, though I do feel that it is imperative the police be contacted as soon as possible."

"I agree. Could I ask a favor of you, Sister, when you do call them?"

"What is that, Mr. Smith?"

"It would be a great help if you'd say nothing about me, or my part in the case, and if you would not mention that Virginia's—" Marco almost spoke the word "mother," then held it back, for it was clear that Vy had not been wholly honest with the nuns at the orphanage. "—that Virginia's guardian is living. They'll assume Virginia has no parents, I imagine. Of course if they put the question to you directly, you'll have to answer."

"Yes, Mr. Smith," the nun replied gravely, "I will."

"With a narrow margin of time in my favor, I may be able to find the girl. Will you help me, Sister Carmen?"

"There is conviction in your tone, Mr. Smith. I want to see Virginia safe again, and if the strategy you describe might bring it about, then I am certainly willing to aid you. Have you an idea about who might have done this terrible thing?"

"I do, Sister, but since time is pressing, let me ask you a question."

In the following moments Marco drew from the nun a restatement of the details Vy had given him over the phone. Sister Carmen also stated that she had sighted a set of fresh tire tracks in the muddy shoulders of the road adjacent to the orphanage grounds.

"Thanks for your help, Sister Carmen," Marco said when she had finished. "Now I suggest you telephone the police as quickly as you can."

"I will do that, Mr. Smith. God be with you in your search."

Marco drained a cup of scalding coffee, flung on his overcoat and left his apartment. He arrived at the Heidelberg Lager manufacturing plant just as the gates opened at eight o'clock. Marco took a chair in the administration building's waiting room.

At eight-fifty, a sleek blonde secretary emerged from an elevator and informed him that Mr. Thiess had just telephoned to say he would not be in his office that day.

"Did you tell him I was waiting?"

"Why, no, sir," the secretary replied. "As a matter of fact, I didn't realize you were waiting to see Mr. Thiess until I called the receptionist to tell her Mr. Thiess would not be here. She said that a visitor was already waiting, so I immediately came down, and . . . Well!" the secretary exclaimed. Marco had already disappeared through the doors.

## CHAPTER XII

Marco raged silently as he pushed the accelerator to the floor and twisted his car through early midmorning traffic. At the city limits, the speedometer needle climbed to eighty. Dim houses shot by, but Marco did not notice. He was fighting with the bitter thought that by aiding Vy Cheyney he was betraying Denis Blaine. Day after tomorrow, Blaine's trial would begin. At best, only one case could be successful. If he located Virginia Brown, Denis Blaine might very well be electrocuted because of it. If he aided Blaine successfully, then Caspar Tolenado might—

Suddenly the rapid-fire voice of the newscaster barked out from the car radio: "And here's a late report just handed to me. Police discovered the body of gangster Caspar Tolenado early this morning in a room in the Edgarson Hotel at 203 Greener Street. Tolenado had been shot through the face. Personnel of the hotel were unable to throw any light on the crime beyond the fact that Tolenado had been registered in the hotel for several days under an assumed name. Tolenado had been sought by police for questioning in connection with a shooting which took place a few days ago in the photography shop belonging to Fritz Rohlwing. Unofficial police sources reported that Tolenado was probably shot to death around three o'clock this morning. The corpse was discovered when . . ."

Tolenado murdered at three in the morning? Then who had kidnapped Virginia?

Marco shot through the gates of the Thiess estate and roared up the drive on shrieking tires. When the butler answered his knock, Marco shoved past. The man followed close behind with a protest. As he moved, Marco loosened his .38 in its holster. He smashed open the doors of the library, stepped through, slammed them loudly shut.

Gregory Thiess gazed up at him from behind his massive desk. Near one wall the stock ticker chattered and spilled its tape across the rug. Thiess seemed stunned. Marco glared at him for a moment, then stalked forward. The butler whipped the door open and burst into the room. Thiess, staring at the detective as if hypnotized, waved the butler to a stop.

Marco said, "Where's Virginia Brown?"

Gregory Thiess awakened like a snake uncoiling. The millionaire's head snapped back and his small blue eyes fixed themselves upon the detective. Slamming his fists on the desk, Thiess growled to the

## THE DEVIL HAS FOUR FACES

butler: "Herrington, get Clyde. Tell him we have an uninvited guest."

The butler darted from the room. Thiess breathed rapidly. A dangerous light flickered in the brewery tycoon's eyes. "Before I have you thrown out of here, tell me your name, so that I may have the pleasure of recalling the man my chauffeur cracked to pieces. Come, come! Speak up."

"Marco Smith's the name. I'm a private detective, working for Vy Cheyney."

"Vy!" Thiess' face mottled an ugly purple. "I might have guessed."

"Look, Thiess!" Marco exclaimed. "You happen to be in a very bad jam. Either come across with your daughter or I blow the whistle."

A muddled expression wiped across Thiess' face. "My daughter?" he babbled. "My daughter? Oh, yes, certainly, as you say, Smith." The fountain of violence shot up suddenly. "Working for Vy, are you? Because of Vy Cheyney I'm in worse trouble than ever before. That makes you partner to that little tramp who's ruined everything." Huffing and wheezing, Thiess lashed out with a large bronze elephant paperweight. The object struck Marco's hand and bashed it against the desk. Marco gasped. Gregory Thiess, panting, yanked the .38 from Marco's inner coat pocket.

A hand snapped on Marco's shoulder, whipped him around to confront the butler, Herrington, and an oafish-looking red-haired young man who bulged from his neatly tailored chauffeur's uniform.

"What shall I do with him, Mr. Thiess?" the chauffeur asked.

"Impress on Mr. Smith that he's not welcome here, Clyde. Impress it on him very strongly."

The chauffeur's face cracked into a grin. "With pleasure, Mr. Thiess."

Anticipating a direct blow, Marco did not respond quickly enough. Clyde hooked a toe around his ankle, seized his shoulders and sent him toppling to the carpet. The stocky man leaped with both feet onto the detective's midsection, then caught a handful of Marco's coat and backed him against the wall next to the stock ticker, where he began throwing punches to his face and belly. Through a reddish haze, Marco overcame pain long enough to shift aside. Clyde's expression changed to wounded outrage as his fist crashed into the wood-paneled wall.

Marco lifted the massive glass bell of the stock ticker and brought it down on the chauffeur's head.

Clyde cried out sharply amid shards of glass. Spitting blood from his lips, Marco snarled, "Someone needs to teach you how to control those dirty hands, little boy."

Defending himself feebly with upraised palms, Clyde allowed himself to be pummeled like a rag doll. Marco knocked him to one side along the wall, then sent him skidding before he had time to sway and fall. Marco cursed steadily, timing each epithet

# THE DEVIL HAS FOUR FACES

to match the crack of fist against flesh. "No, no," Clyde whimpered. "Not any more, not any more . . ."

Doubling his speed toward the door, he slipped and then crawled the rest of the way on hands and knees.

Marco shook his head, spotted Herrington in his line of vision, and lowered his head. Herrington literally flew into the hallway. Marco slammed the library doors and shot the inner bolt. Then he turned and stalked to where Gregory Thiess gaped behind the desk.

Marco removed his .38 from Thiess' limp hand.

"Unbutton your shirt," Marco ordered.

"What?"

"You heard me."

Thiess obeyed, fingers fumbling. Next, Marco ordered him to pull up his undershirt and expose his tanned belly. Then, unstrapping his wristwatch, Marco laid it on the desk and perched on a corner. He wiped blood from his eyes with the sleeve of his coat, and pressed the muzzle of his .38 against Thiess. The brewery tycoon wiggled backwards to escape the cold touch. Marco kept the gun muzzle rammed into the man's flesh. One of Marco's fingers stabbed toward the wristwatch dial.

"In exactly one hundred and twenty seconds, I want to hear what you've done with Virginia Brown, and I want you to take steps to have her returned to Vy Cheyney. Clear?" Marco emphasized his last word by gouging the gun barrel deeper into Thiess' flesh. Flicking his eyes to the dial of his watch, he said, "When the second hand touches zero, you have two minutes to talk or die."

Thiess bluffed sickly: "You—you wouldn't attempt . . ."

"Thiess, I want Virginia alive and unharmed. You have two minutes." Smiling, Marco touched the gun muzzle to the watch crystal and said in a voice soft as death, "Time!"

Thiess gripped the arms of his chair and stared at the second hand inching swiftly in a circle. Marco extracted a cigarette from his pocket with one hand, slipped it into the corner of his mouth. "Thirty seconds," he breathed. "Where's the girl?"

Thiess gargled a series of unintelligible sounds. His eyes appeared to bug from his head. Marco blew smoke into the harassed man's face. Thiess coughed. Droplets of sweat popped out across the expanse of his forehead.

"One minute has passed," Marco said. "Where's Virginia?"

"I can't tell you!" Thiess exclaimed miserably. "Good God, man, believe what I say!"

"Forty-five seconds left."

Thiess shrieked brokenly, attempting to rise. Marco cuffed him sharply and he fell back, gasping for air. He glanced wildly about the library.

"Thirty seconds." Marco rose, stamped his cigarette out beneath his heel, pressured the .38 more firmly into Thiess' midsection. When only fifteen seconds remained Thiess fixed his eyes on the sweeping second hand of the watch. His face purpled until Marco thought he might choke. Ten seconds left. Nine. Eight. Seven. Marco counted mentally, alarmed. If Thiess didn't break . . .

Two seconds.

One . . .

With a strangled shriek, Gregory Thiess fell upon the wristwatch and flung it against the fireplace, where it crashed and lay broken on the hearthstone.

"All right!" he sobbed. "All right, all right, all right!" His head slumped to the desk, and the same words dribbled out of his mouth: "All right, all right, all right."

Marco stepped to a taboret, picked up a water carafe and dumped its contents onto the brewery owner's head. Thiess fought erect, spitting and blinking.

"Settle down!" Marco yelled. He cuffed Thiess once more.

Thiess subsided. His head dropped onto his chest. "I ask you for the final time—where is Virginia Brown?"

"I don't have her," Thiess replied, flinching. "Believe me, I don't have her! If I tell you the truth and you refuse to believe . . ."

A terse note in the man's voice lent conviction to his statement. Puzzled, Marco believed Thiess to be telling the truth. "Did you know Virginia was kidnapped from the Orphanage of Saint Boniface early this morning?" Before Thiess could answer, Marco snapped, "The truth! Did you know she had been kidnapped?"

"Y-yes."

"How?"

"A man . . . telephoned . . ." Thiess wrenched out each word, knowing it damned him. "A man telephoned shortly before eight o'clock."

"Who was he?"

"He called himself Wagner Ulm."

"What did he say?"

"He demanded that I pay him three hundred thousand dollars by midnight, or Virginia would die. If I pay, he will place the girl in my custody and return the original pages from—" Thiess bit his lip, averted his eyes.

"Pages? Return what pages?"

Silence. Thiess breathed noisily.

Marco's stinging slap reported like a gunshot.

"The pages from a book written in German!" Thiess screamed wildly. "A book which shows I donated money to the Nazis during World War Two! Ulm's agent, a moron called Marvel, extorted three thousand dollars from me last night. Then Ulm telephoned . . . to say . . . to say he intended to raise the payment to a one-time lump sum. Three hundred thousand. Before midnight. For the girl and the pages from the book. If I get one and not the other, I'm still ruined. Look—" Crafty in his hysteria, Thiess seized Marco's wrist. "Name your price! Fifty thousand? Seventy-five? For helping me, for keeping quiet—"

Marco's mind raced. The name Wagner Ulm had a contrived Teutonic ring about it. And the mysterious Ulm possessed both the Nazi-donation blackmail information and Virginia Brown. How had Ulm learned about Virginia? Marco thought back rapidly. He remembered the half-visualized figure seated on the opposite side of the pillar behind Vy Cheyney, last night at the French Pheasant. Could that have been the man who called himself Fuchs and Rohlwing and Ulm? How had the blackmailer learned the location of the orphanage? That, Marco could not answer.

Thiess, meanwhile, sat massaging his bruised cheeks and glowering at the detective.

"Did you give the blackmailer a decision?" Marco asked.

"No. I'm supposed to call before noon."

"Call? Where?"

"I—I don't know. A number. If my answer is yes, I'm to say, 'I am coming to the party,' and hang up."

"How'll you know where the transfer of money takes place?"

Dumbly Thiess shook his head. "I have no idea."

"What's the number?"

Thiess pressed his index finger against the top sheet of a memo pad on his desk. Marco took the telephone, dialed the number and then held the mouthpiece before Thiess' face. Marco could hear a recorded female voice repeat tinnily: "This is the Excelsior Answering Service. Please leave the name of the person you are calling, then repeat your message slowly and clearly. Thank you." Thiess hesitated. Marco placed his gun barrel against Thiess' neck.

"I'm calling Mr. Wagner Ulm," Thiess recited. "Please tell him I'm coming to the party."

Thiess hung up. Marco consulted his wristwatch on the hearth, found it intact except for the shattered crystal. The hands stood at five past ten. Marco waved the .38. "Tell your butler to bring in a pot of coffee. We wait for that telephone to ring, Thiess. Neither of us will stir from this room, even if we stay here all day."

Shortly after, Herrington returned with a gleaming silver service. Marco helped himself to a cup of steaming coffee. "Tell Herrington," Marco said to Thiess, "not to entertain any notions about telephoning the police. Although I've got a gun in my hand, I'm your honored guest. Correct?"

Thiess passed a confused hand across his eyes. "Correct." Herrington withdrew, baffled.

Presently Thiess stirred sluggishly. "What are you after?"

"First, recovery of Virginia Brown. Second, Wagner Ulm, the blackmailer."

# THE DEVIL HAS FOUR FACES

"That means my donations may come to light!" Thiess cried softly.

"Too bad."

Thiess showed signs of returning panic. "And Virginia—"

"You made your mistakes long ago," Marco said. "It's too late to rectify them."

At eleven-thirty, the telephone shrilled. Marco lifted the receiver, prodded Thiess in the neck. Thiess spoke haltingly into the mouthpiece. "H-hello?"

"Listen carefully," said a toneless voice. "The party you are to attend will be held this evening at ten o'clock, on the northwest corner of Thirty-fourth and River Streets. Be alone in your automobile with the required amount in bills of denominations smaller than twenty. If you are not on the corner as arranged, or are there in the company of anyone else, the girl and the book are lost. Is that quite clear? Do you understand?"

Marco squinted. What sort of face fitted the voice which whispered out of the wire? Tonight, with luck, he would see the face. Thiess said:

"Yes, I—I understand everything."

The line clicked dead at the other end.

"What happens now?" Thiess wanted to know.

"Wait and see," Marco said. He telephoned the Atlas Bar and Grill.

Twelve-thirty arrived, bringing Harry Soames. Herrington followed him into the library, head bent forward, peering in an oddly outraged fashion at Soames' right-hand coat pocket, into which the ex-detective's hand was thrust. Soames, noticing the stare, withdrew a delicate piece of sculpture showing a shepherd and shepherdess. Herrington did not appreciate Soames' apologetic laugh. "This object belongs on the table in the foyer," Herrington said softly to his employer, and retired. Marco could not suppress a weary grin.

Soames shucked out of his checkered topcoat, rubbed his hands together, then, turning curiously to Thiess, inquired, "Is this gent the job you mentioned over the phone?"

"Right." Marco tossed the .38. Soames caught it deftly. "I want you to guard Mr. Thiess until midnight. Then you can leave. I have an appointment at Thirty-fourth and River Streets at ten, and I don't care to have Mr. Thiess tagging along. Don't let him stir from this room, Harry. He talks to no one—answers no telephone calls, makes none. Only short conversations with Herrington, the butler."

Soames said brightly, "You are the absolute boss. I stick with him until midnight."

Thiess hardly heard. Slumped into his chair, his mind seemed to have drifted off into some unreasonable other world, his eyes rolled up in their sockets. Marco acquainted Soames with the fact that Clyde, the chauffeur, was on the premises.

"Check," Soames replied.

"It's time for me to move along." Marco grinned,

# THE DEVIL HAS FOUR FACES

a hard, cryptic smile. "Wish me luck, Harry. If I don't have it tonight, it won't ever do me any good."

"Luck," Soames called, not certain he understood.

Marco drove back to the city. From a phone booth he called Vy, who seemed calmer.

"Have you been contacted by the police yet?" he asked.

"Yes. A little over an hour ago."

"Um. Did they pry into motives for Virginia's kidnapping?"

"Yes, Marco. But I told them nothing."

"Did you mention Gregory Thiess at all?"

"No. Have you—has anything—" Vy hesitated, clearly afraid to complete the question because it might result in an answer she dreaded.

"Vy, my only lead is thin as a thread. Still, I hope it'll lead me to Virginia."

"Then you have learned something."

"Yes, but I don't want to explain now, in case the lead goes haywire." As it easily could, Marco amended silently. "Perhaps I can call by midnight," he said. "Not before then, so don't expect anything."

Marco hung up, eased out of the stuffy phone cubicle. Nine hours until rendezvous. Already he had begun to sweat, to feel the cold breath of fear in his heart. He returned to the Pacific Minerals Building and began his long vigil. A thin rain began to fall across the city.

## CHAPTER XIII

For seemingly interminable hours Harry Soames had been penned with the disheveled Gregory Thiess in the stuffy library, while rain tapped in a furtive way at the windowpanes. Thiess built a fire, fueling it with several logs so that the air in the closed library became even more oppressive.

Soames never let the .38 slip from his fingers, but as the hours drifted on, he took to gazing idly at books on the shelves, at the broken remnants of the stock-ticker's bell, at any detail of the furnishings which would briefly arouse his interest. He failed to notice the expression of craft which flickered on Thiess' face.

Soames' hands continued to function independently, deftly snitching this and that from around the room, depositing an amazing collection of bits and pieces into his coat pockets. A volume of Boccaccio with four-color illustrations had caught his fancy just at the moment when an ormolu clock chimed half-past six.

Stealthy footsteps made Soames drop the book and whirl in alarm.

Thiess towered up, hefting the elephant paperweight he had wielded against Marco earlier in the day. Soames cried out sharply as Thiess smacked the heavy statue against his skull. The ex-detective plummeted to the floor, groaned once and did not stir. Gregory Thiess swabbed his perspiring face with the back of his hand and bellowed for Clyde.

"Excelsior Answering Service. Please leave the name of the person you are calling—"

"This is an emergency," Thiess broke in. "Is it possible to contact one of your clients? I must speak with Wagner Ulm. I'll pay anything if you'll only—"

"I am sorry, sir," replied the operator. "Our service is based upon the fact that persons being called cannot otherwise be reached when we are answering for them. I will be glad to accept your number and relay your message to Mr. Ulm the next time he checks in, but there is no way we can locate him. Let me check my file a moment . . ." A pause. "Yes, here's the name. Wagner Ulm. No regular telephone number listed. We answer for him on a twenty-four-hour basis."

Thiess muttered, "Tell him to call me at once. If he should fail to check in before ten this evening"—his face twisted in agony as he contemplated the consequences—"cancel the message."

"Very well, sir. Thank you."

Thiess staggered to his private bar and began pouring a large glass of whisky.

At eight-fifteen, Wagner Ulm stepped out of the rain into a crowded cigar store, entered a telephone booth and rang the Excelsior Answering Service, preparing to issue instructions for the evening to the ex-wrestler, Marvel, who checked with the answering service every night at 9:00 P.M. Ulm listened to the operator relay Thiess' message. His lips drew into a tight, merciless line as he hung up, depressed the lever savagely and dialed the brewery tycoon's number . . .

"Understand me, Ulm—I swear to God I'll make the payment. Isn't the very fact that I put in this call proof of my good faith? That's right. Marco Smith will be at Thirty-fourth and River tonight at ten. I tell you he held me at gunpoint and forced me to reveal everything. What choice did I have?

"This way, you can set a trap. And when he's out of the way, get in touch with me. I'll pay; of course I'll pay. How could I possibly double-cross you? You have enough on me to ruin me for life. I want the child, and I want the pages from that book—at all costs." Thiess strove for sincerity, for at last he felt he was beginning to turn Ulm's anger aside.

Ulm hung up, leaving Thiess to wonder whether he would ever untangle the desperate mess of his life. At least, with Ulm forewarned, he had an even chance. Ulm would not seek him out now crying betrayal.

All that remained for Thiess was to release the man Soames in the morning, have Clyde threaten him a bit, and a road would be paved out of the desperate morass in which he found himself. Gregory Thiess retired to his bedroom, took an excessively heavy dose of sedative capsules, and finally fell into a troubled sleep.

Harry Soames awoke in the darkened garage of the Thiess estate. His ankles and wrists had been tightly lashed with many turns of heavy rope. As he shook off grogginess, guilt washed over him. He'd failed Marco Smith. Soames sensed danger for his detective friend. He wracked his brain until he recalled Marco mentioning a rendezvous at Thirty-fourth and River Streets at ten o'clock.

He wrestled with the ropes. His illuminated watch dial showed a few minutes past eight. How the devil could he get free in time?

He breathed tightly, moving his lashed hands, straining to insert fingers of one hand into his pocket. Would there be something . . . ?

He touched glass fragments from the broken stock-ticker bell.

His hands were bleeding when, at twenty minutes past nine, he sawed through the last strand of wrist ropes and went to work on his ankles. At twenty to ten, he broke a window and escaped from the locked garage. He ran around the glowing Thiess house, located his car and went roaring back toward the city forty miles faster than the law allowed. If he failed Smith again . . .

Two blocks from the intersection of Thirty-fourth and River Streets, Marco Smith jabbed the switch that extinguished the lights on his car. Shifting to second gear, he drove slowly along the deserted thoroughfare. Lofts and warehouse buildings reared up blankly on either side, a wilderness where no human roamed after nightfall. Ahead, on the designated corner, an overhead street lamp swaying in the damp wind circled a section of the sidewalk with weak illumination. The hands on the dash clock stood at two minutes before ten. Marco braked at the intersection, twisted the wheel and executed a U-turn which brought him coasting to a stop on the northwest corner, a few yards beyond the periphery of light.

Another .38, secured from his desk, rested on the upholstery against his right knee, where he could seize it quickly. He reached for a cigarette, thought better of it, and leaned back from the windshield as far as possible. Studying the intersection, he failed to see a single person stirring. The illuminated hand of the clock dial showed ten o'clock exactly.

Moments later, a figure stood in the cone of light

# THE DEVIL HAS FOUR FACES

on the corner, hat tugged low and shoulders hunched. Marco's heart began to beat faster as the man advanced toward the parked automobile. A gloved hand tapped lightly on the window. Marco rolled it down carefully, the .38 in his fingers, trying to pierce the shadows surrounding the man's face. A plume of condensed breath shot from his face as the man said:

"So Gregory Thiess sent you in his place, Herr Smith?"

Marco displayed the .38. "Correct. Stand back from the door! When I get out, you climb in."

"Admirable sentiments," mocked the stranger. "But I am not alone, you see. I was forewarned by Herr Thiess of your appearance here tonight. As a result, though I am certain you will not turn your head, on the other side of the car a friend of mine is waiting." Up came a gloved hand to give a light snap of fingers. "Marvel! Inside!"

Marco dared not turn his head for fear of a trick, but when the door on the other side of the car wrenched open and he heard a thick, snuffling breath, he whipped around in the seat and fired point-blank at the misshapen head and shoulders of the giant who had ducked into the car. In the split second before the gun's crash, however, the other man brought a blackjack into play, sapping Marco's arm viciously. The shot went wild, smashing the windshield. The giant Marvel clamped down with his huge hands and wrenched the .38 away.

"Quickly, Marvel," hissed the other. "Use this, then dump him in the rear."

Marco threw a punch at the half-seen giant crowding close. It was like ramming his fist against an iron wall. The huge man chuckled stupidly. One meaty hand around the sap which the other figure outside the car had extended, Marvel arched his arm back and brought the blackjack whipping down to crash into Marco's face. Marco's jaw felt smashed. Marvel clamped a hand on his forehead, pushed his head back and let him have the sap across the bridge of the nose.

Blood gushed from his nostrils as Marco tried to get his hands on his assailant's throat. Rough hands fastened in Marco's hair, snapped his head back once more, and the blackjack crashed against his temple. Then Marvel pushed Marco's head onto the steering wheel and began to beat him rhythmically at the back of the neck. Vaguely he heard a voice shouting, "Stop, you fool! Enough! Enough! I don't wish to kill him yet."

Like a sack of meal, Marco was bundled into the rear of the car and left face down, moaning, on the carpet. Distantly the engine coughed alive. As the car rolled, Marco writhed aside, trying to raise himself. Down came the blackjack. Bombs exploded in Marco's skull, and when the reverberations had died, he heard nothing, saw nothing, felt no pain at all.

# THE DEVIL HAS FOUR FACES

Thick layers of metal seemed to be closed about Marco Smith's brain. A single sound kept repeating; each sharp repetition of the noise setting the invisible metal sheath to vibrating. Marco's head rang like a great bell, excruciatingly. At last the noise broke apart into two words, shouted at close range: "Wake up! Wake up! Wake up!"

Marco opened his eyes and the force of the words slid to an insistent whisper; they had not been shouted, after all. Squinting through dim light, he saw the gray-haired man who called himself Wagner Ulm.

Without thought, Marco reeled to his feet.

Ulm chuckled and minced backward. Marvel shambled into Marco's line of vision, grinning in oafish anticipation. Ulm gestured to the outsized man. "Would you care to go another round with Marvel here, Herr Smith? He is quite willing. Only by sheer force did I prevent him from breaking your bones in the car."

Marco stumbled against a sawhorse, sat down and studied the dim back room of the bookshop, noting with dizzy curiosity the half-painted sword cabinet, a collection of brightly polished sabers, paint cans and brushes. Ulm withdrew to a cabinet along one wall, picked off a Luger and massaged the barrel caressingly.

"This trick is mine, Herr Smith," Ulm said.

"I'm beginning to realize it." Marco's eyes hardened. "The child . . . Virginia Brown. Thiess told me you kidnapped her. Is that right?"

"I removed the child from the orphanage, yes."

"She's alive?"

"Certainly." Ulm indicated a metal ring recessed into a section of the scarred flooring, and Marco, looking closely, made out suggestions of a square trap cut into the wood. "Underneath this little shop is a small cellar area. The child hasn't suffered. I realize you are a detective, but what value can this information be?" Twisted lines of hatred made the man's face writhe. "You—meddler."

Swiftly, Ulm struck Marco three vicious blows in the face. The detective recoiled weakly.

"Don't ever put down that gun. If you do, I'll kill you."

"Bravo, bravo!" Ulm made a play of clapping hands mockingly. "Typical American courage—of the cheap verbal variety. In a few moments, Herr Smith, I intend to let Marvel vent his full strength on you. Then you will have perhaps thirty or forty minutes to live." Ulm's eyes burned into Marco.

"It should delight you to know, Herr Smith, that the instant Gregory Thiess delivers three hundred thousand dollars into my hands, I shall leave this city for another. Quite a few Americans, you see, donated secretly to the cause of my fatherland. All across your nation, these secret givers live out their lives content with the thought that the past is dead, their errors forgotten—if truly they have come to

## THE DEVIL HAS FOUR FACES

see the donations as errors at all. These people I shall visit. Already I would be a rich man," Ulm scowled, "had not you intruded yourself. But now the path to success lies clear. In other cities I shall change my skin as quickly—as easily—as I have done here."

With deft fingers, Ulm slipped out of the false stomach. He unlaced his elevator shoes, kicked them off, turned his head and held his palm forward a moment later. Laughing, he showed Marco a pair of brown contact lenses. He brushed at his white hair, smoothing it into place. Then he picked up a slim book.

"This volume contains the key, Herr Smith. Doubtless you have heard from Gregory Thiess about the information contained in these pages." As if recalling a forgotten idea, Ulm stalked forward without warning and struck Marco in the face again. "Had there been ten thousand more names recorded in these pages, your nation would not have won the war!"

"You're very patriotic," Marco said. "When did you leave Germany—two hours ahead of the American invasion, Herr Fuchs-Ohm?"

The white-haired man chuckled. "My name is not Fuchs-Ohm."

Marco was about to answer when suddenly—shockingly—he knew the words must be true. "Fuchs-Ohm is dead?"

"Yes, in an automobile accident. Burned beyond recognition."

"Then, who are you?"

The white-haired man responded with a short laugh, which stopped as a commotion beyond the curtained doorway caught his attention. Ulm snapped his fingers. Marvel darted from the room while Ulm held Marco with the Luger. An instant later, the giant returned, holding Harry Soames with arms pinned behind his back. Soames saw Marco, tried to speak, but was silenced as Marvel's thick hands clasped over his mouth.

Ulm caressed the Luger barrel. "Well!" he said softly. "Two shall die, instead of one, then."

Marco said softly, "Harry, why in hell did you turn up here?"

Unable to speak, Soames muttered from behind Marvel's hammy hand. Ulm gestured broadly, using his Luger. "Oh, let them talk a few moments. After all, when two human beings are about to have their lives extinguished, they should at least be allowed a moment of companionship." Ulm's chuckle sent a chill down Marco's spine, but at the same instant he conceived an idea for escape. He repeated, "How did you wind up here?"

"If this gorilla will let go . . ." Soames struggled, but Marvel only gripped him harder.

Marco, listening for a certain sound, barely heard it. He hoped Ulm had not noticed.

# THE DEVIL HAS FOUR FACES

Marvel released his hold on Soames when Ulm waved for him to do so.

Soames straightened his coat collar and began:

"Thiess hung one on my head. Next thing I knew, I'd been trussed up and thrown in the garage. I managed to get rid of the ropes, and then I remembered you said something about an appointment at Thirty-fourth and River. I landed there a couple of minutes after ten, watched your car drive off, and followed. The street outside is pretty dark, so I couldn't tell whether you came in here voluntarily with these two jokers. I hung around a few minutes, then decided to barge in. I figured by then that you were in trouble."

"A masterful understatement," Ulm purred.

"I wish to hell I had telephoned the police," Soames blurted.

"Have you ever seen our host before?" Marco asked. "Think carefully."

Soames frowned. "No, never. Wait a second, though. He halfway looks like . . . Yeah! That photographer. What was his name?"

"Rohlwing."

Soames nodded. "There is a resemblance."

"But he isn't Richard Fuchs, the magician? The man who hired you to blackmail Andrew Strauss?"

"Absolutely not."

Ulm threw back his head and laughed. "You shall wonder when you go to the grave, Herr Smith. This is perhaps the choicest illusion of my career. My name is indeed Ulm, but it is also Rohlwing. My name is neither Fuchs nor Fuchs-Ohm, yet I am all four. But enough." The Luger barrel swung decisively. "Herr Smith, you and your friend will advance to the wall and stand facing it." Marco and Soames obeyed. Ulm tossed the Luger to Marvel, bent and hefted one of the sabers beneath the sword cabinet, testing the weapon's keenness against the ball of his thumb.

"Raise your hands!" he exclaimed suddenly. "Up high, over your heads!"

Marco obeyed, half-swung his head, caught Soames' eye as he framed the word: *"Pocket."*

Soames scowled, indicating he did not understand. Sweat leaped out on Marco's forehead. *"Pocket,"* he mouthed. *"Pocket!"*

Soames' eyebrows shot up.

Behind the two men Ulm spoke softly: "In a moment or two I shall end your miserable lives by a thrust of the saber through your spine into a certain vital area of your body. This principle was the first taught to all Prussian officers, because it combines sureness of death with a maximum of pain."

Breathing hard, Marco realized that Soames had understood the message. His eyes flicked downward; he licked his lips. Soames nodded imperceptibly.

"And thus I say farewell, my meddlesome gentlemen."

# THE DEVIL HAS FOUR FACES

The last words were accompanied by a grunt of physical effort as the saber drove home.

Marco leaped one way, Soames another. The saber buried itself in the wall inches from Marco's ribs as Soames ripped an object from his pocket and hurled it into Ulm's face. Marco clamped his hand around the saber hilt, wrenching the weapon from the wall. Ulm uttered a cry as a glass-and-metal salt cellar struck him on the forehead.

"Watch Marvel!" Marco called sharply.

The brute, both hands around the Luger, raised it and fired.

Marco dodged down and lunged forward before the giant could fire again. With arm extended, he rammed the saber through the giant's shoulder, pinning him to the wall. Marvel brayed with pain as Marco ripped out the bloodied weapon, seized a light packing case and flung it at the giant's head. Marvel reeled through the door, clutching the curtains as he fell.

Soames cried out a warning, and Marco turned to see Ulm rushing at him with another saber.

Marco felt the blade tear through his side like a tongue of fire. Harry Soames snatched up the Luger and triggered two shots, bright orange fire spitting through the gloom. Ulm whipped his arm down and the saber came free of Marco's flesh. Ulm teetered backward, his legs corkscrewed beneath him and he tumbled to the floor.

Marco leaned on the sword cabinet for support. Harry Soames mopped his forehead.

"That ring," Marco pointed. "A trap door. Pull it."

Soames obeyed, revealing a black maw from which issued a stale, unpleasant odor. Marco heard faint sobbing from below. Soames knelt at the trap's edge. "Why, there's a kid down here . . . a little girl! Come on, don't be scared. Take my hand. That's right. Up we come . . ."

Weak from loss of blood, Marco crawled toward the prostrate Ulm, who stared up in terror, realizing that the moment of death was drawing close. Marco felt Soames clutching his shoulder.

"Mr. Smith, you need a doctor—"

"Call an ambulance," Marco muttered. "Hurry! Don't—don't bother me, Harry. I need—to talk to Ulm before—"

Soames darted from the room, carrying the frightened Virginia in his arms.

Marco leaned forward, supporting himself on his arms, and gazed down into the ashen face of the dying man.

"Who are you?" Marco gasped.

The dying man's eyes closed. He bit his teeth against pain. Then the white-haired man said softly, "My name is Erwin Kloder."

## CHAPTER XIV

The report which Marco Smith typed thirty-six hours later on the battered Underwood in his office in the Pacific Minerals Building was later submitted to Diana Meadows, then read by Vy Cheyney, Andrew Strauss, Denis Blaine, Assistant District Attorney Leland Comstock, and—with grudging admiration—by Captain Brainard.

Marco typed the report with one hand. His other rested in a sling, one of many bandages applied to him by hospital personnel.

Through his office window a clear blue winter sky sparkled above the rooftops of the city, yet Marco could not erase from his mind the image of the dying man's face as he whispered in the back room of the little bookshop. The blackmailer lay stiff in death on a morgue slab now, yet he remained vitally alive in Marco's mind as the latter laboriously pecked out the story.

The report, in part, ran:

> General Reinhard Fuchs-Ohm of the Nazi High Command apparently never awakened to the fact that in the heart of the one person he trusted most implicitly, his stolid, ever-faithful aide, Erwin Kloder, lay the seeds of his own destruction. In the last analysis, Kloder was perhaps a more ruthless opportunist than his general, for when the occasion arose, Kloder did not hesitate to turn upon the man whom he had served faithfully for many years; the man whom he had followed into self-imposed exile halfway across the world, through Switzerland, Algeria, Colombia, Mexico, and finally into the United States, on a fortune-hunting expedition whose very scope staggers the imagination.
>
> True, Fuchs-Ohm was quite willing to sacrifice Kloder to save himself, or at least the story which Kloder gave to me in his dying moments indicates this. Fuchs-Ohm carefully planned his campaign of blackmailing Nazi sympathizers by means of the German book smuggled out of Berlin and turned over by me to Captain Brainard of the police department. Fuchs-Ohm's scheme had been set up months, even years, ahead of time. Kloder, on the other hand, knew only an instant's warning of betrayal.

It took him just that instant, according to what he told me, to realize he had been played for a fool, and that it would be very simple for him to step behind the masks Fuchs-Ohm had so carefully established; step behind them and finish the blackmail plan after Fuchs-Ohm died. Kloder, of course, killed Fuchs-Ohm and placed his body in the automobile which was wrecked and burned on the highway.

The exact route which this Quixotic Nazi and his opportunistic Sancho followed to our city, we shall never know. Kloder briefly sketched the route—given above—before he died. Fuchs-Ohm must have had a fund of cash large enough to establish himself in America after several years in other countries; money to purchase forged papers and set up the three blind fronts behind whose screen he could operate, changing appearances at will: the tiny magic shop of Fuchs, the photo shop of Rohlwing, the bookshop run by Ulm.

In each case, Fuchs-Ohm, according to Kloder, manipulated a simple prearranged disguise which instantly altered his appearance. For the character of Fuchs the magician, he used no disguise at all. For playing Rohlwing, he planned pads of wax to fill his cheeks, a brown toupee, and very thick glasses. For the character of Ulm, he obtained a strapped affair which, when put in place, gave him an immense stomach. A pair of elevator shoes and brown contact lenses completed the change.

Fuchs-Ohm would not have made such elaborate preparations if he had not been sure of gaining more than a substantial return on his obviously large investment. Glancing over the Nazi record book now in the hands of the police convinced me that Fuchs could literally have been a millionaire several times over, had his plans not misfired. There are not a great many Americans listed in that book, but there are enough—wealthy ones—to have made a rich killing.

The police have confiscated the book and eventually, I imagine, they will deposit it with the proper group in Washington.

Why did Fuchs-Ohm set up his three blinds so intricately? The very fact that Kloder, using the identical blinds, eluded capture for so long is justification enough. Kloder, of course, was able to switch roles and take up where Fuchs-Ohm left off because physically he resembled the general very strongly. Denis Blaine viewed Kloder's body yesterday and remarked about the same thing.

Which brings me to the evening of the party at the Strauss mansion. Fuchs-Ohm had already sent Harry Soames to make blackmail overtures to Andrew Strauss. Why, then, did he insist

# THE DEVIL HAS FOUR FACES

upon carrying out such a dangerous maneuver as entering the house of his blackmail victim to put on a performance as a magician? Cross it off to the man's sheer nerve, and perhaps an insatiable desire to watch Andrew Strauss secretly, a wish to examine the first victim of his labor; to watch, in effect, the butterfly caught and skewered on the pin.

What a blow when Fuchs-Ohm confronted Denis Blaine, a man he believed he had left dead in an attic in Berlin years before. I imagine Fuchs-Ohm instantly conceived the plan to make Fuchs the magician appear to "die," implicating Denis Blaine at the same time and thus putting a stumbling block in the path of further investigation.

I know from Kloder's words—who heard it from Fuchs-Ohm before the latter died—that after Denis faced the general in the kitchen of the Strauss estate, Fuchs-Ohm opened his shirt and, with nothing but desperation to kill the pain, plunged the blade of a carving knife about a quarter inch into his body. Then he folded his magician's robe over his shirt and went out to perform what he hoped would be his finest illusion. Fuchs-Ohm had been, at one time in Germany, a professional magician.

The bullet-catching effect was performed by Fuchs in the way used by most magicians who are willing to tackle it at all. Denis Blaine marked the bullet. Fuchs-Ohm had palmed a small tube, closed at one end, the outside of which exactly duplicated the pattern on an ornamental ramrod he used. After inserting powder and wadding into the pistol, and tamping both down with the ramrod, he dropped this tube into the muzzle. Thus the bullet landed in the tube. While appearing to ram home the bullet a final time, Fuchs-Ohm actually engaged the tiny tube with the ramrod, extracted both. No spectator, of course, ever noticed the slight additional length of the rod.

Customarily, the magician turns, walks to his target position, palms the bullet from the tube and slips it into his mouth. This time, Fuchs-Ohm did not follow the procedure. He let Denis Blaine fire, whipped open his robe as if in pain, and revealed the blood on his shirt front caused by the knife wound. Then he fled from the Strauss home, climbed into his car, drove to some public telephone and called Kloder.

Fuchs-Ohm ordered Kloder to meet him on a deserted stretch of road in the Briarwood suburb. To account for the time lapse before the planned accident, Fuchs-Ohm knocked at the door of Dr. Massilon. Dr. Massilon, frightened, refused to let him in. Imagine the pain Fuchs-Ohm must have withstood. But he did not genuinely expect Massilon to take him in. As a mat-

## THE DEVIL HAS FOUR FACES

ter of fact, he probably would have run away if the doctor had consented to treat him.

Thus Fuchs-Ohm drove to the rendezvous. Kloder had taken a taxi from the city. He climbed into Fuchs-Ohm's car on the lonely stretch of road—and found a Luger pointed at his head.

Fuchs-Ohm explained calmly and dispassionately that Kloder had to die to make it appear that the magician had perished in an automobile accident. Thus Fuchs-Ohm could slip into his next disguise as Rohlwing, and pursuit of the magician would stop.

Fuchs-Ohm explained his plan quickly, swaying weakly from loss of blood. Kloder wrenched the Luger from his hands and knocked him unconscious.

Fuchs-Ohm had requested Kloder to bring a small black case from the magic shop, a case which contained a mate for the muzzle-loader which Fuchs-Ohm had left at the Strauss mansion. Fuchs-Ohm had described the six-pointed star marked on the bullet by Denis Blaine. Kloder simply marked a bullet in the way Fuchs-Ohm described, fired it from the muzzle loader into the already-wounded Nazi, drove the car along the highway and sent it careening over.

Kloder, the intended victim, then slipped behind the screens already set up by Fuchs-Ohm, and, with the bitterness of betrayal still seething in his mind, set out to blackmail prominent citizens exactly as Fuchs-Ohm had planned.

My clue to the switch was Soames' failure to recognize Kloder after the latter stripped off his disguise in the bookshop. Soames had met Fuchs-Ohm posing as the magician, but he did not recognize the photographer or the book dealer.

As for other pertinent details of the case . . .

Marco completed the report, slipped his coat across his game arm, switched out the light and moved slowly toward the elevator, a look of concern worrying his face.

Andrew Strauss fretted in his swank office on the top floor of the Strauss Brewery administration building. How soon would his father appear? Already it was eleven o'clock. Since finding the morning paper neatly folded as usual on his silver breakfast tray, Andrew Strauss had trembled in fear. Spread in glaring headlines and a three-column lead for the entire city to see was the story of the death and capture of Erwin Kloder, the blackmailer.

Strauss had slipped quickly from the house and come to his office, to set his papers in order and pre-

## THE DEVIL HAS FOUR FACES

pare for the worst. No employee except the guards in the gatehouse had been on duty at his arrival. The guards, however, had watched him covertly, knowing his guilt, snickering.

Jerked alert by the rasp of the intercom box on his desk, Andrew pressed a cam and said in a shaky voice, "Yes?"

"Your father is coming in, Mr. Strauss," his secretary said. Andrew mopped his forehead. Subtle nuances in her voice told him that she, also, had read his name in the columns of the morning newspapers. The door to his office crashed open and old Karl Strauss towered above him, looking like an avenging god.

"I read," Karl Strauss breathed softly. "Your shame is mine, and is now littered before the public."

Andrew attempted to speak. No reply came forth.

"Had I known where you were sending decent money during the great war," Karl Strauss breathed, "I would have shot you to death, although you are my own son."

"What shall I do?" Andrew whined. "What do you want me to do? Leave the country? Go to South America?"

Livid, Karl Strauss slapped his son full in the face.

"*Nein!* You shall not run! You shall stand and face the charges! If there is prison, so be it. When you aided those gas-oven butchers you cut yourself off as my son. You shall stand and face the bitterest punishment which the law can deliver. I do not care what becomes of you. I only say you shall not escape punishment."

The old man stamped from the office.

That evening, as Andrew Strauss drove through the plant gates between crowds of departing workers, from out of nowhere a rock was hurled against his windshield. Glass spattered against his cheek. Blood dotted his shirt collar. Suffering all the agonies of the damned, he pushed his car through the crowd and, like a robot, drove not to where he wished to go—anywhere, away—but toward his father's home in Briarwood. He could not flee, and he realized it.

Perhaps, he thought suddenly, perhaps in time, I may be able to expunge the blot and again be considered human. In the midst of a bleak world, the thought gave him a very tiny amount of cheer.

That same morning Gregory Thiess had emerged from his own bedroom and eaten a light breakfast, noting Herrington's rather odd stare. While leaving the dining room, he passed his wife. Her birdlike appearance and wizened body revolted him even more than usual. Bent in her wheelchair, crocheted motto lying in her lap, she peered at him with her customary vapid smile.

# THE DEVIL HAS FOUR FACES

"Gregory, dear. Will you take me to church soon?"

He passed on without a reply.

He locked the library doors behind him, read once through each account of Kloder's capture, paused a moment over his name where it appeared in print, and then took a small pistol from a wall safe. Herrington came running as the burst echoed through the house. He had to call Clyde. Together they broke down the door and found the body.

Diana Meadows waited impatiently behind the wheel of Denis Blaine's automobile. At last the doors of City Prison opened and Denis emerged. Diana's heart quickened. How haggard he looked, yet smiling, as Captain Brainard walked part way down the steps with him. Brainard had a very embarrassed expression on his face as he shook Denis' hand.

Denis turned and sprinted for the car. He threw open the door and Diana was in his arms, both of them oblivious to the stares of pedestrians passing the parked car.

The tiny Porsche spun up the long hill toward the Orphanage of St. Boniface. Marco drove, Vy beside him. Suddenly she pointed.

"Look! There's Sister Carmen in front. With Virginia . . ."

Through dazzling sunlight, Marco saw the nun and the little girl waiting. He turned to Vy.

"Made up your mind?"

She smiled, touching his arm. "I—I think so. At least I want to try. No more beer industry. Just you and my daughter."

Marco said, "There is a better than even chance that we'll end this in Reno, in six months or a year, Vy."

"If we want to make it work . . ."

"As I do," Marco replied.

"Then let's take the chance!"

He smiled and braked the Porsche. Sister Carmen came forward, smiling. Virginia Brown, a charming, warm-eyed little girl, hung back.

Marco Smith suddenly found himself with a grin across his face. He helped Vy from the car, stretched out his hand and said—almost shyly—"Hello, Virginia."